WINGED NURSE

Avis Leigh was a special kind of nurse in West Australia. She was also a licensed pilot, and covered an area of three hundred thousand square miles, flying from day to day into the remote bushland to take medicine to the settlements and missions in the wilderness. Hers was a lonely fight against disease, a ceaseless struggle against time and distance. Her ruling passion was flying, with nursing a very close second, until two men entered her life. Both appealed in their different ways, and Avis knew love for the first time, but it took a near-disaster to clarify the situation.

WINGED NURSE

Winged Nurse

by

Helen Berry

Dales Large Print Books
Long Preston, North Yorkshire,
BD23 4ND, England.

British Library Cataloguing in Publication Data.

Berry, Helen
    Winged nurse.

    A catalogue record of this book is
    available from the British Library

    ISBN   1-84262-309-5 pbk

First published in Great Britain in 1970 by Robert Hale Ltd.

Copyright © Helen Berry 1970

Cover illustration © Michael Taylor by arrangement with
P.W.A. International Ltd.

Published in Large Print 2004 by arrangement with
Robert Hale Ltd.

Dales Large Print is an imprint of Library Magna Books Ltd.

Printed and bound in Great Britain by
T.J. (International) Ltd., Cornwall, PL28 8RW

CHAPTER ONE

Avis Leigh narrowed her blue eyes against the glare of the Australian sunlight and peered ahead as her tiny single-engined plane neared the bumpy airstrip at the Blue Ridge Mission. When she saw the two-engined plane on the ground she knew Ralph Curtis was delivering supplies, and her heart beat a little faster as she circled to land. She saw a group of natives standing by the cluster of buildings to the side of the airstrip, and a smile touched her tanned face. She made a good landing and taxied in, and for a moment she sat glancing around before stepping out. This scene was all too familiar to her, but she wouldn't have changed it for anything in the world.

A crowd of native children came swarming towards her as she got out of the plane and carried her large medical bag towards the mission. She was surrounded by laughing, gesticulating children, and a large boy snatched her bag and carried it off in triumph. Father Conrad Wayland, who ran the mission, came towards her with a smile on his weathered face.

'Nurse Leigh, we've been expecting you for the past hour. It's amazing how these people know you're coming.'

'Bush telegraph, I expect, Father,' Avis retorted with a smile. She was a slender, pretty blonde, and the last two of her twenty-six years had been spent flying around the stations, missions and settlements in the remotest corner of West Australia, attending to the thousands of aborigines living there. She had been a nursing sister in a large coastal hospital, in comfortable surroundings but with little time for flying, which was her all-consuming passion, until she had been unable to endure it longer. Her suggestion to the West Australian Department of Health that a nurse with an aeroplane might be of more value operating in the northern bushland than occupying her present position had been welcomed with surprising eagerness, and so Avis combined both her loves, nursing and flying, and found her life most satisfying.

'I've got some problems for you, Nurse,' Father Wayland said.

'As usual,' Avis replied. 'But nothing serious, I hope.'

'Since you showed me what to look for in the eyes I have been carrying out clinics every week,' Father Wayland said seriously. 'I have found several cases of trachoma. They are waiting for attention now in the clinic.'

'Have you used the drops I left?' Avis demanded as they walked towards the buildings.

'I've used it all,' came the swift reply. 'The children are very co-operative. I've had to use the eye-dropper filled with clear water on those children who aren't affected, because they're so disappointed when they don't get the treatment.'

'That's a good idea, Father. It gets them used to being treated when the need arises. I'll have a look at those children first, then start giving out the sugar cubes.'

'You're doing a wonderful job, you know,' Father Wayland remarked. 'I've never seen these people looking happier. It's a red letter day when you are due to visit.'

'I'm so glad. The facts do justify my existence.'

'But it is so wearing upon you. It's a pity there aren't more like you, Nurse.'

'There couldn't be another like her, Father,' a cheery voice called from an open

9

doorway, and Avis turned quickly to see Ralph Curtis emerging from the store. He was grinning widely, his bronzed face showing great pleasure. 'Hello, Avis, this must be my lucky day. I've been trying to land on the same airstrip at the same time as you for days, but all my calculations are wrong. Today I never expected to see you, and here we are together.'

'Hello, Ralph, how are you keeping?' she demanded, smiling, and her heart seemed to increase its beating for a moment. Ralph Curtis was a tough man, rugged and powerful, although he was no taller than Avis herself. His blue eyes were incredibly pale, and a shock of very fair hair hung down over his forehead.

'Too busy for comfort, like you,' he retorted. 'Are you staying long?'

'About four hours.' Avis glanced at her watch. 'I've got some sugar to hand out here.'

'It beats me how the kids clamour for attention,' Curtis said. 'Before you started this round, Avis, you couldn't get them near a doctor.'

'Nurse Leigh is unique,' Father Wayland said. 'It will be a sorry day for us when she decides to marry and leave us.'

'I have no intention of doing that, Father,' Avis replied quickly. 'I'm much too busy for romance and, anyway, I've never yet met a man who interests me.'

'That's bad news for me,' Curtis said, grimacing then smiling. 'I thought I was making real progress, Avis.'

'You're too like me to want to consider romance,' Avis replied. 'You'd rather be flying than on a date with a girl.'

'But a date with a girl who flies is another thing,' he retorted. 'You really ought to have been a man, Avis, with your passion, although I'm extremely grateful that you're not.'

'Why can't a girl have such a passion and yet seem normal?' Avis demanded. 'There are hen birds, remember, and have been as long as there's been male birds.'

'Sure, and they go well together,' Curtis said, laughing. 'I think that's a good sign for me, don't you, Father?'

'I'm sure Nurse Leigh will know the right man when he comes along,' came the steady reply.

'Well, all right. Perhaps we'll have the chance for a talk before I take off,' Curtis said. 'I'm just about finished here now. Will you be taking a break in half an hour, Avis?'

11

'I'll see if I can spare the time,' Avis replied. 'But if I can't, then happy landings, Ralph.'

'Thanks.' He shrugged fatalistically. 'The only way a man can get to see you is by falling ill. It's something I haven't considered before, but you may find me as a patient one of these bright days, Avis.'

'I hope not,' she retorted. 'I like seeing you around, Ralph.'

'Thanks.' He grinned and went about his business, and Avis entered the small clinic, where a native nurse, unqualified but willing to do the menial tasks and handle the slightly sick, came forward with a wide smile upon her dusky features.

Seven children were awaiting attention, and Avis washed and put on a clean overall. The first of the children came before her and Avis examined the child's eyes, peeling back the lids to search for the tell-tale white spots which are trachoma, a highly infectious corneal ulceration of the eyes to which aboriginal children are extremely susceptible. The virus is aggravated by sand and dust, is extremely painful, and eventually causes blindness.

'That is bad. You must take drops every day,' Avis said, and the youngster grinned widely, happy at the thought of getting treated. The other six children were as badly affected, and Avis saw to their treatment. Father Wayland joined her shortly, and she sighed as she spoke to him. 'I'll take out the time to look at all the children, Father,' she said. 'How many are there?'

'Forty-three,' came the reply. 'Do you want them in now?'

'Yes please, and afterwards I'll administer the antipoliomyelitis vaccine.'

'They're already beginning to queue for that,' Father Wayland said. 'It's better on sugar than as an injection. We don't get so many tears this way.'

Avis agreed. Anything that saved her time was a valuable aid. She had a set routine for treating the natives, whether she was visiting homesteads, missions, schools, hospitals or clinical centres. Her operating area covered a vast three hundred thousand square miles of outback, and apart from her medical duties she had to maintain her aeroplane herself. She was an accomplished mechanic, as Ralph Curtis found out once when he had engine trouble on a small airstrip in the back of beyond and couldn't pinpoint the trouble. Avis still pulled his leg about that on the few occasions when she wanted to

13

change the subject when in his company. She had located the trouble in three minutes and put it right while he was on the radio trying to summon aid.

It took her three hours to attend to the patients at the mission, for in addition to checking the children for trachoma she had to inspect their feet for hookworm, administer the pink Sabin antipoliomyelitis vaccine which was soaked into sugar cubes, and inject the younger babies for diphtheria, whooping cough and tetanus. By the time she finished her duties Ralph Curtis had long since gone, leaving a message for her with Father Wayland. As she was preparing to leave, Father Wayland came to her with the message, and Avis smiled as she listened to the Father's gentle but insistent voice.

'You and Ralph are two of a kind, Nurse,' he said. 'Two people I am always very pleased to see here at the mission and not just because of the good work that you both do. I know you take more than a professional interest in the people, Nurse Leigh. You're a very special person in all our hearts.'

'I always do what I can, Father,' Avis replied, glancing at her watch. 'But now I must hurry and leave you. I have to call at the Bartlett homestead. Mrs Bartlett isn't well, and Matron asked me to call in on her some time today.'

'I haven't seen the Bartletts in three weeks,' the Father replied. 'I do hope it isn't serious.'

'I don't think so. There's a child on the way. It's her third, so she's used to the procedure now.'

'Give them my best regards, please.' Father Wayland accompanied her to the airstrip, and all the children of the mission followed noisily.

'I'll do that, Father.' Avis turned and waved to the children, and there was an outburst of cheering as she climbed into the cockpit. She stowed away her bag and prepared to take off. This particular moment was always exceedingly pleasant for her, and the great sigh of relief which she gave as the wheels lifted from the bumpy strip had nothing to do with the fact that she had just finished a tiring stretch of duty. It was wonderful to get free of the earth. She checked her course and flew north, but by now she knew almost every square mile of her territory and didn't need the compass. Her mind was clear and pleasantly relaxed as she flew on towards the Bartlett homestead.

She was made welcome wherever she went, and her landing in the meadow beside the Bartlett house brought Tom Bartlett out in a hurry. There was a cheery grin upon his bronzed face as she climbed out of the plane to greet him.

'Hello, Nurse. Glad you could drop in. The wife is feeling a bit dicky, and I thought it better that someone should take a look at her. I'm glad they asked you to call instead of the flying doctor.'

'Doctor Ramsey wouldn't like to hear you say that, Mr Bartlett,' Avis retorted in friendly fashion. 'How is Mrs Bartlett? What seems to be the trouble?'

'She's feeling very ill, and thinks she ought to be in hospital. She thinks she's going to lose the baby.'

'I see.' Avis unconsciously quickened her step as they walked towards the house. 'Has she been doing too much?'

'As usual.' Bartlett was a tall, lean man in his early forties. 'It's no use trying to tell her to ease up. She's like a flaming idiot when it comes to work.'

'It's a hard life for a woman,' Avis conceded, 'and I expect Mrs Bartlett has more than enough to do. How are the two children?'

'Fine. Nothing to report as far as they're concerned. Freda goes to school now, you know, and is liking it.'

They entered the house and Avis went into the bedroom to see the patient. A cursory examination confirmed Mrs Bartlett's fears, and Avis nodded as she considered.

'I don't think I'd better leave you, Mrs Bartlett,' she decided. 'The doctor would call tomorrow if I sent in a message, but that may be too late. I'm on my way to Kalarra now, so if you'd like a trip in the aeroplane I'll take you in on the way. You'll have to go to hospital, and the sooner I get you there the better.'

'A ride in your aeroplane!' Mrs Bartlett was a small, thin woman, her hands and face showing the rigours of her life here in the wilds. 'I'd like nothing better, Nurse. But is there enough room for two in it?'

'We can squeeze in. I often carry passengers when I'm a bit pushed. Perhaps you'll pack a case with your immediate needs, and while you're doing that I'll go down to the plane and radio the hospital to let them know you're coming.'

'Thank you, Nurse. I don't know what we'd do without you being able to drop in like some bird of mercy.'

Avis smiled as she departed. It was on occasions like this when she realised her

17

worth to the community and the medical authorities, and the knowledge never failed to give her a wonderful sense of justification. She explained the situation to Tom Bartlett, and his face fell as he listened. But she hastened to reassure him.

'You've got nothing to worry about, Mr Bartlett. I want to take your wife in as a precaution.'

'I understand, Nurse. Is there anything I can do?'

'Not right now. As soon as Mrs Bartlett is ready I'll be taking off. I'll just let the hospital know what's happening, and to expect us.'

'I'll chase her up, and say goodbye to her,' he retorted, and went back into the house with a grim, purposeful expression on his weatherbeaten face.

Avis went to the plane and radioed her base, giving the information she had and estimating her time of arrival at the hospital field. By the time she was ready to leave Tom Bartlett was bringing his wife out of the house, carrying a small suitcase in one large hand, the other upon his wife's shoulder.

'Are you sure this thing is safe for the both of you?' he demanded anxiously as they helped the woman into the machine.

'Don't worry,' Avis told him with a smile. 'I've carried a sixteen stone man in here with me. Mrs Bartlett doesn't weigh that much, does she?'

'Not even in my present condition,' the woman said cheerfully. She was looking forward to the experience of flying, and Avis knew she wouldn't have any trouble with her on the flight.

They were quickly airborne, and for a few moments Mrs Bartlett couldn't speak. Avis circled the homestead, and the tiny figure of Tom Bartlett could be seen waving furiously.

'Are you all right, Mrs Bartlett?'

'Fine, thanks, Nurse. This is wonderful. I didn't know it could be so exciting.'

'One never really gets used to it,' Avis admitted. 'I'm only happy when I'm up here.'

They flew south-west, towards the coast, and all too soon for Mrs Bartlett they sighted the large town of Kalarra, where Avis was based. As they landed an ambulance drew up at the side of the field, and the plane had hardly come to rest before Mrs Bartlett was being transferred to the ambulance.

'Thank you, Nurse, for everything,' the woman told her. 'That trip was just what the doctor ordered.'

'I'll come along and see how you are later, Mrs Bartlett,' Avis promised, and the woman waved a hand as she was taken away. Avis sighed and relaxed for the first time in many hours. For a moment she stood still by the wing of her aircraft and looked around. Her eyes ached from the glare of the sun, and her shoulders and legs were protesting at the ceaseless activity in which she had been involved since early morning. She took her bag and case out of the plane, and as she looked around for some means of getting to the main hospital building a mile away she spotted a car coming towards her. She nodded as she recognised it as belonging to Doctor Ross, and tried to steady the sudden gyrations that unaccountably affected her breast. It was as if her heart had suddenly doubled the rate of its beating, and the effect was breathlessness and a feeling of unsteadiness that left her unbalanced and tottery. But she knew what caused it, and the knowledge afforded her much gratification.

'Hello, Avis, I was hoping you'd show up soon.' Duncan Ross opened the door for her, and got out to lift in her bag and case. 'I heard you were bringing in Mrs Bartlett, and I'm hoping you'll be finished for the day.'

'I'll have to check with Matron,' Avis said. 'But I've done everything that was on my schedule this morning. I hope I'm through. I feel very tired.'

'That sounds ominous,' he remarked, his face turning serious. He was a tall, huskily built man of twenty-eight, dark and handsome, and he had been getting friendly with Avis for some weeks. At first she had rebuffed him as she did all men, but recently she had been relaxing her stiffness because there was something about him that attracted and appealed. She had even been out with him on a date, and he had been trying to get her to repeat the experience ever since. She was looking forward to the opportunity, but so far her duties had kept her away from Kalarra at the time he was free.

'Don't take any notice of that,' she retorted. 'I'm always tired.'

'I'm not surprised, the amount of time you spend zooming around the bush. You're some bird, Avis.'

She smiled as he drove to the hospital buildings. She liked his manner and the way he talked. Because he was a doctor, part of their interests were the same, and they talked shop on that first date and never got off the subject. He hadn't tried to kiss her, and for that she was thankful. She'd never had any time for romance, and the quickest way to lose her friendship was for a man to try and get amorous. But he had only wanted to be friendly, and she was keen to repeat the date, but she wasn't showing him her eagerness.

'What about this evening then?' he demanded as he halted the car.

'What about it?' she teased. Her blue eyes shone brightly in her tanned face.

'I'd like to take you out. We could go for a drive, have a bite to eat somewhere, then talk.'

'All right.' She nodded. 'But let me check with Matron first. It wouldn't be the first time she asked me to run out on an extra job.'

'I'll wait for you,' he promised. 'But I checked with Matron half an hour ago and she said there was nothing else on the schedule for you.'

'You're beginning to get organised!' She smiled into his intent face. 'All right, I'll be ready to go out at around seven-thirty. Will that do you?'

'Fine.' He nodded eagerly.

'Nothing strenuous,' she warned. 'I'm ready to curl up in a quiet spot with a good book.' For a moment they stared at each other. Then she sighed. 'I'll have to take a look at the plane before I can call it a day. Next week I'm due for a full service. I'm getting through a great number of miles now.'

'I'd like a flight in that machine of yours, but I'm afraid to ask because it will be too much like work for you. You're flying all day and every day.'

'I like any excuse to fly,' she retorted. 'What about this evening? Would you like a flight?'

'I certainly would.' His eyes glowed for a moment, and Avis nodded as she took her case and bag from the car.

'All right, so meet me on the strip whenever you're ready. I shall be down there checking up on the engine.'

He nodded and drove away, and Avis stood watching his departure for a moment. There was something about him that undermined her determination to stay well clear of romantic entanglements. Her well-ordered life had no room in it for a man, someone whose presence might start demanding time and thought. She was afraid that a man might cause too much havoc for her to continue her present way of life. She'd seen the changes that came to some of the nurses when they fell in love, and she didn't think she could exist under such restrictions and burdens.

She sighed again as she entered the hospital, and she dumped her bags in the duty room and went along to Matron's office. Tapping at the door, she tried to climb down from the heights of her lonely day's nursing. She was always exalted by the time she got through. Her job was not like normal nursing with strict, crippling routines to follow. There was always some large programme of preventive medicine to be operated, and she saved the flying doctors a lot of work by operating as she did. When she heard Matron's voice inside the office she opened the door and entered.

Phyllis Anson was a woman of forty-two, bright and modern in her manner and approach to nursing. She had accompanied Avis several times on her trips into the bush, for no more reason than that she thoroughly approved of Avis's work and wanted to know more about it, plus the excitement of flying. Avis liked the matron extremely well, and they got along together.

'Anything else for me to do, Matron?'

'Avis, I'm glad you came in.' There was a frown upon Miss Anson's gentle face. 'I heard you were on the way. How is Mrs Bartlett?'

'Fine in herself, but I'm afraid she's going to lose her baby,' Avis replied.

'Sit down, please. There's nothing else for you today, but I would like to go over tomorrow's schedule, if I may.'

'Certainly.' Avis sat down and relaxed, but she could feel her hands trembling slightly, and there was an eagerness in her breast which hadn't been apparent before she landed. Knowing that her date with Duncan had brought on the feelings made her even more nervous.

'We've scheduled two jobs for tomorrow,' Matron said, smiling as she regarded Avis's taut face. 'Sabin vaccine for the Sweetwater settlement and booster injections of three-in-one for the babies at Ookawurra. Can you manage that?'

'If I make an early start I shall be able to get through by evening,' Avis replied, making a few calculations.

'I'd like to come with you,' Miss Anson said, sighing regretfully. 'But I'm too busy here to spare the time. If you had a nurse

25

with you there'd be more time for you, Sister. I worry a lot about the volume of work that's being thrust upon you.'

'If the doctors had to do it a lot of the sick patients would not get treated,' Avis said. 'I'm taking some of the non-urgent jobs from them to relieve the pressure. It's only right that I work to my capacity.'

'I'm glad you look at it like that,' Matron said, shaking her head. She was a tall, slim woman, dark and vivacious, not anyone's idea of a hospital matron. 'We'd be in a bad way now, after coming to depend on you, if you suddenly decided to stand up for your rights as a nurse.'

'I'm not likely to do that,' Avis said with a smile. 'I'll be ready to take off at seven in the morning. That should give me enough time to handle both jobs. I'll be in at six to check the supplies. Will that be all right?'

'Fine,' Miss Anson said, nodding firmly. 'Happy landings, Avis.'

Avis smiled as she departed, but she quickly forgot about the next day's schedule. As she went to her quarters she was already thinking of her date for the evening, and a thread of pure excitement was stitching in her mind. Thoughts of Duncan Ross were uppermost.

CHAPTER TWO

Duncan Ross arrived at the strip just as Avis was finishing off her inspection of the aeroplane, and he stood looking on with interest as she replaced an inspection panel and jumped down off the wing. She wiped her hands on a cloth, watching his face for reaction, and was pleased that he seemed content that her occupation was out of the ordinary. Some men regarded her as an odd fish when they learned how she spent her time – not so much for the nursing side but that she flew an aeroplane and knew how to maintain it.

'Everything all right?' he demanded.

'Just fine,' she replied. 'Park your car over there and give me a few minutes to clean up and I'll be ready.'

She liked the expression of anticipation that crossed his lean face. But as she went to wash up she wondered just what she was starting. If she became too friendly with him it might lead to all sorts of complications. She was happy enough as she was, with her work and her aeroplane, without taking on added interests and perhaps asking for trouble. But she felt the need for a complete change of atmosphere, and Duncan's company seemed the right relief to her at that moment.

He was walking around the plane when she returned to it, and he smiled as he turned to her.

'Let's get in,' she said. 'Have you ever been up before?'

'I haven't, but I think I'm going to enjoy it. I thought about taking up gliding, but that's about as far as it's gone, just thinking about it.'

'I belong to the gliding club here,' Avis said. 'If you are that interested then I'll be happy to take you up and teach you all about gliding.'

'You would?' He nodded enthusiastically. 'Then I'll gladly take it up, if only to get out and about in your company.'

'You wouldn't stick it long if you didn't have a real interest in gliding,' she told him. 'Let's see if you like it the next time we're free together.'

'A good idea! I couldn't have suggested anything better myself.'

They got into the machine and Avis took

off. She felt the customary thrill at the moment of lift-off, and breathed deeply. She climbed steeply, and circled the hospital, giving Duncan a good look at where he spent most of his days. He was smiling, intent upon what he saw, when she glanced at him.

'This is great,' he commented as they left the town behind and headed out over the bush. 'No wonder you never get tired of flying, Avis.'

'You like it?' She flung him a glance.

'Very much. I'll take you up on that gliding offer.'

'This and gliding cannot be compared,' she said. 'But I love both forms of flying.'

'And I'm sure to take to it,' he retorted. 'But only if you act as my teacher.'

They went for a short flight, and after an hour Avis set the machine down on the airfield again. As they alighted Duncan took her arm. His eyes were shining as he told her how much he had enjoyed himself. Avis was touched by his words. There was a new respect in his eyes, and she felt a thrill touch her with intangible fingers.

'Let's go eat now,' he said. 'The Dingo Club will suit us. Then we'll talk about flying.'

'You certainly know the way to a girl's heart,' Avis told him. 'But please remember that I have to be up at around five in the morning. I shall be taking off at seven.'

'Another heavy day?' he demanded as they got into his car.

'A couple of jobs to handle. But it will take me all day.'

'Doctor Ramsey was telling me yesterday what a relief it is to have someone like you taking most of his routine jobs off his back. If ever a girl found herself the perfect occupation, Avis, it's you. Where did you get this love of flying from?'

'My father, I expect. He's president of the Alton-Leigh Airlines.'

'Really! I didn't know that. I suppose he was in the Air Force during World War Two!'

'Yes!' She nodded. 'That was something I wish I could have taken part in. It must have been wonderful to fly against a well-equipped enemy.'

'You're a strange girl, Avis!' He shook his head as he drove into town. 'I've never met a girl like you. You're so different from other girls of your age.'

'I'm sorry about that,' she replied.

'No you're not,' he retorted boldly. 'And I'm glad you are different. We can have a lot of fun together.' He paused and glanced at her, then added cautiously, 'but that's if you don't mind my company. Tell me if I become too much for you. I know you're always doing everything alone, so if you get too much of my company then tell me so and I'll go drown myself.'

'I'll remember that,' she told him with a smile.

They had dinner in the club, but Avis found a strange restlessness gripping her. Being in Duncan's company for only two hours had done something to her. She felt as if she were being drawn by a large magnet, and there was such a tingling sensation inside her that she believed he had hypnotised her in some obscure way. When they left the club the shadows were long and clearly defined, and Avis sighed heavily as she emptied her mind for a moment and let the thoughts of the next day assail her.

She was beginning to like her off-duty periods, and Duncan was strictly to blame for that. There was a little gathering of awareness inside her mind that festered like a sore foot. She was becoming too aware of him! It had been bound to happen, she knew, and had warned herself against it, but despite the knowledge of what would happen she had gone into an involvement regardless. She knew that, and was secretly satisfied by it. Romance was about the only human activity into which she hadn't plunged with her characteristic fervour and enthusiasm, but even now she was contemplating it, and the knowledge in itself was surprising, but she wouldn't find a better man for the experience, she thought remotely, glancing at him as he drove slowly back towards the hospital.

Soft darkness was falling about them when the car halted near the large Nurses' Home, and the stars were large and looked very near. Tiredness was settling upon Avis, but she kept fighting it off, hoping against hope that Duncan would make up his mind to kiss her. Suddenly she wanted very much to be kissed, and an air of unreality settled upon her like an unaccustomed cloak. She suppressed a sigh as she prepared herself mentally for his action, but he sat watching her, on his own side of the car.

'What's it like up there among the stars?' he demanded.

'Wonderful,' she replied, smiling. She stared at his face, but his expression was hidden in shadow. How many times had she kept a man at bay by talking of flying when he wanted to kiss her? The thought flitted through her mind like a big butterfly. Now the shoe was on the other foot, she thought, nodding. She wanted Duncan to kiss her and he was talking flying. 'I'll take you up one night,' she promised. 'But now I have to be getting in. It's a hard life for a girl.'

'But we will go out again?' he demanded, leaning towards her, and Avis felt her pulses race.

'Of course! I've thoroughly enjoyed myself this evening.'

'You're just telling me that. After flying all day I made you take me up for a flight.' He laughed softly.

'It depends who you're flying with,' she said firmly.

'Then you liked my company?'

'Now you're fishing.' She laughed merrily. 'Let's say that if I didn't like your company wild horses wouldn't drag me out with you again.'

'That's a relief to know. You've been an extremely difficult girl to get to know.'

'Was it worth all the effort?' she demanded. Her heart was beginning to beat faster. She could feel a tightening in her breast, as if her emotions were being wound up too tightly. Her throat had an emotional lump in it and she found her breathing beginning to quicken. She had never felt like this before, unless perhaps it was when she had been learning to fly. But that had been a few years ago and she had forgotten all about the tensions of getting to know something she had loved. But the sensations were all back as if they had never left her, and they were present only because she had been with Duncan.

'It was more than worth the waiting and scheming,' he replied. 'I can tell you now. I switched duties and did extra duties just to be free when you were, but all to no avail. But it was all worth it just for this evening. Let's hope it will be all plain sailing after tonight.'

'I think it will be.' She spoke softly, and there was a husky note in her tones. She was aware that he moved closer to her, and she looked up expectantly. He was just a blur in the night, but she could hear his breathing, and saw his hands coming towards her. She felt like a swimmer about to meet the biggest wave of all, and took a deep breath as he gathered her gently into his arms. His mouth came out of the darkness, touching her cheek before finding her lips, and Avis shuddered a little and closed her eyes, sinking into an unfamiliar welter of warm emotions. It was a kiss such as she had never experienced before. It drew her and overwhelmed her, and filled her with such unaccustomed passion that she felt panic rising in her breast.

'Avis, I don't want to scare you off,' he whispered, stroking her hair. 'It's taken me such a long time to get to know you. But I have a great deal of feeling for you, and I want you to know that you'll never regret the day you decided to get to know me.'

'I'll never regret it,' she replied softly. 'I have enjoyed your company tonight, Duncan. I shall be looking forward to the next time.'

'And I'm very happy that there will be a next time,' he said joyfully. He kissed her again, and there was some urgency in his lips. She felt herself responding naturally, and the old familiar feelings of repression and wonder were already fleeing from her consciousness. A strange and powerful emotion was beginning to invade her, and she shivered at the acknowledgement she made to it. Her breathing quickened and she trembled. When he kissed her again she experienced such passion that it frightened her, and when he released her she felt as if she were in a dream as she got out of the car.

'Goodnight, Duncan,' she said waveringly.

'Shall I see you tomorrow?' he demanded.

'I don't know what time I shall be getting back,' she mused. 'But you'll know when I arrive, won't you?'

'I'll know,' he said. 'Good night, Avis, and sleep well. I shall be thinking of you all day tomorrow.'

She smiled at him and went in to her quarters. Sitting before her dressing-table mirror, she stared at her flushed face and gleaming eyes as if the face of a stranger confronted her. There was an inner trembling affecting her breast which she had never experienced before, and there was a heat in her cheeks and a burning sensation in her lips that was thrilling and wonderful. She could still feel the strength of his arms about her, the pressure of his mouth against hers, and her senses seemed to gyrate, as if she had been too long on a merry-go-round.

Sleeping seemed impossible when she got tiredly into bed, but as soon as her eyes closed she drifted quickly into unconsciousness, and the next morning the alarm clock awakened her from deep sleep and she sat up in bed with a sense of anticipation gripping her. Her mind was filled with shrouds of sleep, but cleared as she recalled the previous night. Her cheeks flamed as she remembered how Duncan had kissed her! Would she ever be able to face him again?

Then her feelings got the better of her embarrassment, and she got out of bed to dress. She didn't wear the traditional uniform of the nurse when she was on duty. A short skirt and a blouse was more than sufficient in the heat and the closed cockpit of the plane. But this morning she put on a colourful dress, and there was a song in her heart as she breakfasted and listened to the local weather report. The day was going to be bright and dry, and Avis was satisfied as she prepared to make a start.

She was at the hospital at six, checking the plane and then the medical contents of her case and Coolite box. By seven she was ready to depart for the Sweetwater settlement. Her two jobs were straightforward, but she never knew what would be awaiting her arrival. Apart from her scheduled work she always checked the children for trachoma, and handled any medical situation that came along. She planned to go to the settlement first, then cut down to Ookawurra to complete her day's work. With her gear safely loaded into the plane, she checked with the office to see if there were any additional orders, and satisfied that there were not she went back to the airstrip and got into her plane.

For a moment she sat staring ahead, lost in thought, her mind living in the past of last evening. There was a mixture of new emotions in her breast, and she almost squirmed as they attacked her. What on earth was happening to her? There was a pain in her throat where emotion gathered, and her hands were trembling as she prepared for take-off. Could love affect a girl like this? Did it affect every girl in the same way? She shook her head as she tried to clear her mind. This was one of the things she had against romance. A pilot needed a clear mind, especially a pilot who was also a nurse with a great many things to do and a lot of distance to cover. But she wouldn't have missed the date with Duncan for anything in the world.

Taking off, she left behind her a great deal of the thoughts, and the old familiar lightness filled her. She envied the birds with their ability to fly free and unburdened, but this was the next best thing, and she counted her blessings as she set course for the Sweetwater settlement. There was a long trip ahead of her, and she settled down to the day's work, still having to fight against her personal thoughts, now crowded into the back of her mind.

The morning was bright and clear, and Avis felt her spirits lifting like a kite. One could ask no more from life than that happiness attended every action. Her work was her hobby! She was indeed fortunate to be able to combine her two loves in this way, and she tried to peer into the future as she winged north-east. How long would she be able to continue in this way? For two years she had been sublimely happy. The future hadn't seemed to matter at all so long as she could keep flying and nursing. But there were other considerations to be made. Life was short, so very short when all the facts were considered. She was now twenty-six, and she smiled to herself when she conjured up a picture of herself at fifty, climbing in and out of an aeroplane. Would she be a confirmed spinster, wedded to her work, embedded in her rut of routine so deeply that she would be unapproachable in other matters? She shook her head, suddenly dissatisfied with what she had thought would be a golden future, and there was a picture of Duncan Ross in her mind.

So that was it! She sighed deeply as her

mind opened and showed something of the turmoil going on beneath the surface. There was a strange, dragging sensation in her breast, and she knew it stemmed from attraction to Duncan. A lump came to her throat as she recalled the wonder of his kisses the previous night. She wouldn't have believed it possible if she hadn't experienced it personally. No wonder girls would do anything for the man they loved! It was a revelation to her.

There was little to do but think as she flew through the bright sky, and usually she thought about her work and what it entailed. But this morning her mind was filled with Duncan, and she kept taking a deep breath as emotion built up inside her. She was looking forward to the next time they would go out together, not so much for his company as for his embraces and kisses. Her cheeks flamed from time to time, and she was startled by the impulsive desires that thrilled through her. Something strange had been awakened in her breast, and she could not fight it or control it.

The bushland passed by under her wings, flat and featureless, deserted for the most part, with homesteads here and there, filled with loneliness and unreality. Avis didn't need her compass in this area. She knew exactly where she was, and her blue eyes glinted as she looked around her for her next landmark. A glance at her watch and a check upon her instruments informed her that all was well, and she continued, filling slowly with tension as the time passed, because she didn't know when she would be seeing Duncan again.

Would it be possible to see him that very evening? She sighed as she considered the many long, hot hours stretching before her. It was unusual that she should concern herself with the work ahead. She loved nursing, and the long hours had never mattered before. She breathed deeply, only part of her mind on her flying.

But a part of her was alert, for suddenly she stiffened and swung the plane in a tight circle. Her narrowed blue eyes had spotted something unusual on the ground. She frowned as she went back, searching for the object again, and then she saw it, and a gasp spilled from her as she recognised the shape of a crumpled helicopter in the bush.

Sweeping in low, Avis stared down, and saw a motionless figure lying yards from the crashed machine. She turned again, going very low, and this time she called her headquarters on the radio, giving the position of the incident. It didn't seem safe for her to land, but she knew help was needed instantly. When a reply came over the radio, informing her that a local police helicopter had failed to report in, she knew she had found the machine, and again gave her position.

Gaining altitude, Avis flew over the area again, looking for a place to land and, picking a spot, she swooped down for a closer look. There was a flat stretch that seemed almost suitable, although it was barely long enough, but she set her teeth and went in easily, ready to pull out at the last moment if necessary. But she made it comfortably, coming to a halt a quarter of a mile from the helicopter. Taking her medical bag, she hurried through the bush towards the scene of the mishap, arriving there breathless and soaked with perspiration.

There was a second man, she saw as she neared the crash. He was still in the crumpled machine. Avis dropped to her knees beside the nearest man and examined him, but a cursory glance was sufficient to see that he was beyond her aid. He was dead! The second man lay in the helicopter, caught among the twisted body of the machine. Avis had to pick her way through the wreckage to get near enough to check him. She fancied he was dead, but to her surprise he was still alive, though badly injured. She gave him an injection of morphine and examined him for injuries. There was a tight frown upon her face as she discovered that both his legs were broken and he possibly suffered a fractured skull. She dared not attempt to move him, and after making him as comfortable as possible she sat down to await the arrival of aid.

As the time passed she became impatient. The man needed urgent medical attention...

Later, she heard the throbbing of an engine, and got to her feet and peered skywards. Almost immediately she saw the large hospital helicopter whirling towards her, and the pilot picked out the crash with no difficulty at all. The machine came down quickly and easily, landing only a few yards away, and Doctor Ramsey and Nurse Eden alighted, hurrying towards Avis. The pilot emerged and unfastened a stretcher, which he brought to the side of the crashed helicopter.

'It was fortunate that you spotted this, Sister,' Doctor Ramsey said. He was carrying out an examination as he spoke. 'You managed to get down all right?'

'Yes.' Avis nodded. 'He's in a bad way, isn't he?' She reported what she suspected, and Ramsey quickly diagnosed the same injuries.

'We might be able to save him,' he said, 'if we can get him back to Kalarra in time.' His hands were busy as he spoke, and Nurse Eden helped him. They worked as a team and Avis knew she would only get in their way if she tried to help. Ramsey looked up at her. 'Don't run away yet, Sister,' he said. 'We heard a report over the radio that a police helicopter is on its way here. They'll want to talk to you.'

Avis glanced at her watch and nodded. She moved away from the scene and stood talking to the helicopter pilot until Doctor Ramsey was ready to move the patient. Then they all helped to transfer the man to the stretcher. A few moments later the stretcher was attached to the helicopter and the machine was lifting rapidly and whirling away back in the direction from which it had come. Silence settled slowly, and Avis sighed. She could understand illness, and death was a frequent visitor among her patients. But accident was another thing altogether, and she could never face the prospect of it without an inward shudder.

The heavy silence that hung over the bush seemed to have a depressing effect upon her, and Avis stood listening for the first sounds of the police helicopter. She felt as if she were suspended in time, and the sensation was uncanny. Even the exalting thoughts of Duncan Ross could not cover over her shock at finding this wreck, and she wondered what had happened to the mechanical bird that it should plummet out of the bright sky with such deadly results to its passengers...

CHAPTER THREE

By the time Avis heard the approaching helicopter the loneliness of the bush was getting on her nerves. She scanned the sky for first sight of the machine, and saw it coming down fast to land close by. It picked the same spot the hospital helicopter had, and two men alighted, one dressed as an inspector of the police. Avis recognised him as he came grimly towards her. It was Inspector Temple.

'Hello, Sister Leigh,' he greeted. 'Thank you for spotting this. It must have been quite a feat from the air.'

'It was lucky I had to fly over the area,' she replied.

'I got the news over the radio that one man was dead and the other is in a very bad way.' Temple studied the scene with a professional eye. 'But this is out of my field, I'm afraid. We'll have to get an expert out here to find out what went wrong. I'm sorry you had to wait around for me, because you're always so busy.'

'I shall be late, too, today,' Avis said, glancing at her watch. 'But this sort of thing cannot be avoided.'

'I shall need a statement from you,' Inspector Temple said. 'But if you're in a hurry I can catch you some other time.'

'You'll have more luck catching a horsefly, Inspector,' she retorted. 'Better get your statement now.' She gave a brief account of what had occurred and he wrote it down in a notebook.

'I'll accompany you back to your machine,' he said. 'You only just got in there, didn't you?'

'I usually allow myself more room,' she admitted.

He took her bag for her, and they walked through the bush to her machine. Avis checked the strip she needed for a take-off, then boarded the craft. The inspector stepped back to watch, and she taxied forward and soared upwards like a bird. She flew back over the inspector, and he waved, and then she picked up her course and resumed her interrupted journey.

Now she was ninety minutes behind schedule, and she flew steadily through the trackless sky, her thoughts busy with more urgent problems now. Personal life was nonexistent! She had rolled it up like a carpet and stored it into the back of her mind. Soon the collection of buildings that formed the Sweetwater settlement came into view, and there was a crowd of people anxiously awaiting her arrival. They had been informed of her visit, and the estimated time of her arrival. Now they were concerned that some mishap had befallen her! She swooped down, scaring the chickens and small livestock, and landed safely.

She chocked the nosewheel of the plane and locked the cabin, and there were more than enough helpers to carry her box of refrigerated vaccine to the ramshackle hut that was the local clinic. A count of the people awaiting the Sabin vaccine totalled almost two hundred, and Avis enlisted the help of the local nurse to get the pink vaccine into the sugar cubes and thence into the mouths of the aborigines. An hour later she was checking the children for trachoma and hookworm, then turned her attention to the babies who needed the injections against tetanus, whooping cough and diphtheria. As soon as possible she was in the air again, heading for Ookawurra, and she felt a little easier as she guessed that she had made up some time.

The heat was terrific as she flew on. A haze shimmered over the bush, and the sky was brassy, cloudless and without mercy. The glare made Avis squint her pale eyes, and she was breathing shallowly. But this was only early summer, and there was a lot worse heat ahead of her. When she landed again she was limp with weariness, her strength sucked out of her by the sun. She attended to her duties, and just before five in the late afternoon she was free to return to Kalarra. She did so thankfully, looking forward to a refreshing shower and a change of clothes. But in the back of her mind was the hope that she would be seeing Duncan later, and this thought alone pushed her on when she felt like resting.

Kalarra was a welcome sight when it showed on the horizon, and Avis started her descent to the airstrip. She landed safely and unloaded her cases. A car came out to meet her, driven by one of the porters, and she was conveyed to the hospital building. A check with Matron's office proved that her day was over, and she signed out with relief. Her legs ached, and she felt as if her veins were filled with fire as she walked slowly towards the Nurses' Home. But she stiffened when a voice called to her, and she turned swiftly, all thought of tiredness gone when she recognised Duncan's tones. He was hurrying towards her, his face alive with eagerness.

'Avis, it's been a long day,' he started, then lapsed into silence and stared anxiously into her face. 'You look dead beat,' he went on. 'I'd better not ask you out this evening.'

'Why not?' she demanded. 'It was the thought of seeing you this evening that kept me going all day.'

'Really?' His eyes lit up with inner fire. 'That makes a difference then. But I'll make it a simple evening, shall I, and won't let it finish too late?'

'You're very thoughtful.' Her eyes showed her pleasure, and he lifted a hand to her shoulder in a gentle indication of his feelings. 'How is that policeman they brought in this morning?' she queried.

'He died in the operating theatre, poor devil. There wasn't much chance for him, despite the fact that you spotted that crash. You don't close your eyes up there, do you?'

'I wouldn't last very long if I did,' she replied, smiling wryly. 'But we'll talk later if you like. Right now I'm dying for a shower.'

'I'll see you at around eight,' he said. 'I shan't be able to get away much before then. But we can go out for an hour or so, just to break the monotony of the day, and I'll see you get to your bed early. What have you got on for tomorrow?'

'One trip so far, and it isn't a long one.' She smiled. 'I want to know how Mrs Bartlett is. Can you tell me?'

'She's the miscarriage you brought in yesterday!' He thought for a moment. 'I have it. She lost the baby, but she's all right herself. She can go home tomorrow.'

'Can she? Well I shall be passing pretty close to her home, so if you're going back on duty now, Duncan, perhaps you'll ask her if she'd like a lift. Otherwise she'll have the

50

devil of a job to get back.'

'She did mention it to me,' he said, smiling. 'I said I'd ask you about it, but it slipped my mind when I saw you.'

'That's a bad sign. You'll have to watch yourself, Duncan, or I shall be getting the blame for any mistakes you make, not keeping your mind on your work.' She was smiling, for thoughts of him had intruded into her work all the day through, and she knew a tremor of wild hope as she realised that he was suffering the same sort of thing. Did he have that wonderful, feathery sensation in his chest? If he did could it mean that he found her very attractive? She studied his face while they chatted for a moment longer, and she knew without doubt that he was the nearest she had ever come to finding a man who fitted the image of the dream man in her mind. It was a satisfying knowledge! It filled her with unassailable hope. It lifted her above her tiredness.

'I'll go back now and have a word with Mrs Bartlett. What time will you be flying out tomorrow?'

'I want to check the plane first,' she replied, thinking hard. 'About nine-thirty, I suppose.'

'I'll see that she's ready to leave at that time, and telephone the information to her home so they can expect her. See you later, Avis.' He squeezed her arm gently and turned away, and after watching him for a moment she turned and went on to the Home.

A shower was the first requirement, and she flung off her limp clothes and pulled on a dressing gown. When she stood under the cold water she closed her eyes and relaxed, and the thrumming streams of refreshing water against her smooth skin was like a gentle caress. She stayed almost too long under the water, and was cold when she emerged, but a brisk towelling restored her and she dressed in a lightweight skirt and blouse and sat down to recover her vitality and energy. She didn't feel much like eating, but a meal was a necessity and she went to the large dining-room. As she sat eating the meal she listened to the light-hearted chatter of the off-duty nurses around her, and she felt a pang of nostalgia touch her.

She was leading a lonely sort of life! She missed the association of these cheerful girls. Her job was as important as theirs, if not more so, but they worked as a team, whereas she was on her own.

What had brought on the feeling she did not know, but she left the dining-room as soon as possible and went to her quarters, intent upon catching up with her personal chores. She kept an eye on the time, but had an hour to kill before meeting Duncan. She felt restless and unsettled as she finished off her work and considered getting ready to meet Duncan. Then on an impulse she went to the telephone and put through a long-distance call to her parents' home in Perth. Her mother answered, and Avis felt happier at the sound of her voice.

'Hello, Mother,' she said. 'How are things at your end?'

'Avis, it's good to hear your voice! I was thinking of you this afternoon, and wondering if I could reach you.'

'Is there anything wrong?' Avis demanded.

'Nothing wrong, but it seems so long since we last saw you. Father was thinking of flying us up to Kalarra this week-end. But then you're always busy, weekend notwithstanding. When are you coming home to see us?'

'I'll think about it. How's Father?'

'Busy, as usual. My family is a rare one for working. How are you keeping?'

'Quite well, Mother. I've made friends

with one of the doctors here, and when I come home next time I'll arrange to bring him with me.'

'That's good news, Avis. I've been wondering when you would get around to it.'

'Don't start thinking those thoughts, Mother,' Avis warned, but she was smiling, her good spirits restored. 'I'll try and arrange for the week after next, but it will really depend upon Duncan's duties.'

'Any time that will suit you will be all right, Avis. You're not working too hard, are you?'

'Not too hard!' Avis pulled a face at herself as she spoke. 'I like to keep busy, as you know.'

'How's your flying?' Mrs Leigh asked the inevitable question.

'Still sailing along. I suppose Father is as bad, isn't he?'

'I can't keep him on the ground. He's supposed to be behind a desk, as you know, but at every opportunity he's in a cockpit instead. It's a wonder they get any paperwork done in his office.' Mrs Leigh laughed indulgently. 'But I ought not to talk to you about trying to remain on the ground. You've had your head in the clouds for a very long time.'

'It's the best place to be,' Avis retorted instantly. 'It isn't so crowded up there.'

'But I sometimes forget that I have a daughter,' her mother complained. 'I wish you were living nearer home, Avis.'

'I don't live all that far away, by flying time,' Avis replied.

'But I can't fly a plane, and your father can never find the time to bring me to you.'

'I'll try and get home more often if you like,' Avis told her.

'That would be nice. I lead a lonely life, Avis, despite the fact it's you out there in the bush. But don't let it worry you. I know you're very busy. But it's a job that has no ending, isn't it?'

'That's true!' There was a rueful note in Avis's voice. 'It's like trying to get water from a well in a bucket that's got a hole in the bottom. But the main thing is, we are improving the standards of health generally, and that's to be applauded. A few more years at the present rate and I shall become redundant.'

'I don't think that appeals to you, but if it ever happened you would go off somewhere else to begin all over again.' Mrs Leigh sighed. 'But I mustn't be selfish, Avis. I must take comfort from the fact that I brought you up.'

'You did a good job on me, Mother. Are you sure you're all right? You sound a little bit depressed.'

'I'm all right. If you're all right then everything is going well. But I'm glad you telephoned, Avis. It's nice to hear your voice again.'

'I'll ring more often, and I'll see about the week-end after next, Mother. But I shall have to hang up now. Take care of yourself and give my love to Father.'

'Goodbye, dear. Get some relaxation now and again, won't you?'

'I promise,' Avis said, and reluctantly hung up. She sat for a moment, thinking of her mother, and then she sighed and finished dressing. By the time she was ready she had to hurry to meet Duncan.

The sight of him, wearing a lightweight suit and looking very smart and handsome, drove all other thoughts out of her mind, and Avis caught her breath as he came to her and took hold of her hands.

'You're looking very beautiful, Avis,' he said.

'You're looking pretty smart yourself,' she countered. 'I shall have to watch my appearance in future or I might let you down.'

'Don't ever worry your head with that

thought. You look as if you've just stepped out of the pages of a fashion magazine. And you don't look so tired and strained now, Avis. I think you are working a bit harder than you ought, you know.'

'I felt shocked today by my discovery of that crashed helicopter,' she replied slowly. 'That upset me. Usually I can skip through my day.'

'Well, I shan't keep you out too late,' he retorted firmly. 'I don't want to be blamed if you crack up.'

They got into his car and left the town. Avis sighed and relaxed, breathing deeply. She looked around at the familiar scenery for a bit, then glanced at Duncan's lean face. She told him about her telephone call to her mother.

'She suggested I go home the week-end after next,' she said casually. 'Can you get off duty at the same time?'

'And go with you?' he demanded, glancing at her. His brown eyes were shining with eagerness. 'I'd like that very much. But you'll have to return the favour.'

'How?' She could guess what was coming, but hadn't heard anything yet about his personal background. He hadn't mentioned his parents.

'We'll go home to your parents as you suggest, and the next time we're both free we'll take a trip to visit mine. What do you say?'

'I'll agree, if you'll tell me about your parents,' she responded with a smile.

'Yes!' He nodded. 'For all you know my family might still be living in a cave.'

They both laughed, and Avis felt very happy as he drove on.

'My father is a lawyer,' he said at length. 'Another very busy man! The world is full of people like us, Avis.'

'My father is another,' she replied. 'Mother was telling me on the phone that she's awfully lonely.'

'Everyone is lonely at some time in their lives. My mother has the same complaint. It's having to work that makes the men seem so remote. But I think you'll like my parents. They're very homely, and they've been on at me for months to take home a girl.'

'I've had the same trouble with my parents. They want me to take home a man.'

'And you think I may fill the bill?' He eyed her for a moment.

'I think you'll do for the time being,' she replied with a laugh.

'And you may help me to get my parents

off my back for a bit. Let's make a pact over that, shall we?'

'I'll do anything you suggest,' she told him.

The rest of the evening seemed to fly away, but they had been late meeting, and Avis felt a pang of disappointment when Duncan turned the car around and quite firmly started back to town. She sat motionless at his side, and when he parked in a lonely spot she quivered with anticipation. He took her gently into his arms, and at the contact of their lips she knew without doubt that whatever happened in future, she would never be able to forget him. He had come closest to her idea of a perfect man, and she had never felt the urge to be loved until the previous night, when he had taken her into his arms.

Her outlook upon life had changed completely in the past twenty-four hours, she realised. A new set of values had taken hold of her, and she could not fully understand all the significances of what was happening.

'Avis,' he said softly when they drew apart later, 'I must tell you that getting to know you is the most pleasant thing I've ever done. I watched you for a long time before I could get around to asking you out. You seemed so complete in yourself that I hardly dared to interrupt your life.'

'Well, I'm human, for all my appearances,' she said with a smile. 'How do I differ from other girls?'

'I wouldn't be able to answer that from experience,' he retorted. 'I was never one for gallivanting. I've always kept my nose to the grindstone. It's always been the other fellow going out on dates, and that sort of thing.'

'I've been practically the same,' she volunteered. 'But I've always had my passions for flying, and sometimes riding, but that only to a lesser degree.'

'And yet you've settled to nursing,' he mused. 'You're a mixture of several things, Avis.'

'I hope that's not bad.'

'Certainly not. I've never come across a happier or more accomplished girl in my life. The work you're doing in this area is tremendous, and your way of doing it accomplishes more than the previous official methods.'

'My personality?' she demanded, and he nodded seriously. She sighed to relieve the emotion filling her. 'Well, so long as I'm justifying my presence,' she said, and shrugged her slim shoulders.

He glanced at his watch. 'We never seem to be together long,' he observed. 'A day is like an age, but the evening passes in a flash. It must be you, Avis. You put a spell on me and all sense of earthly things vanishes. I don't know what to expect next.'

She watched his face, shadowed now by the growing darkness of approaching night. There was a curious lightness in her breast as she picked out the features of his countenance. There was a deeply graven image of him in her mind, and each passing moment added to the depth of it. She was aware that he had an overwhelming effect upon her. She felt helpless before the surging emotions that were loose inside her. She had little idea of what was happening in her mind. There was such a turmoil. But she was aware of new and powerful sensations that were not unpleasant, and she was happy in the knowledge that he was attracted to her. For a girl who had never found time for romance she was beginning to understand many things fairly easily.

'Is it time to go?' she demanded reluctantly, and he nodded.

'I'm afraid it is. Shall I see you again soon, Avis?'

'Whenever you want to!' There was a glint

in her blue eyes as she spoke, and he reached out and gently followed the line of her cheek with a gentle finger.

'Tomorrow evening?' It was a question, and she nodded instantly.

'I shall have to find the time to service the plane,' she said.

'Perhaps you can do it while I'm with you. I won't mind watching you instead of going off somewhere. I want to spend as much time as possible in your company. Do you mind that?'

'No!' She stirred as her breast was assailed by many strong emotions. 'I look forward to seeing you, Duncan. I realise now that I've spent so much time on my own. My days are lonely, apart from the stops I make, and until we started seeing one another I spent my evenings with the plane.'

'You can have too much of that,' he retorted. 'I think I'll make it my task to see that you do get some relaxation now and again. You could crack up if the pressures continue ceaselessly.'

'Thank you, Doctor.' There was a smile on her lips, and he leaned towards her and kissed her firmly but gently before he sighed and started the car. Then he started back to town, and he was filled with the knowledge that at his side sat the most important girl in the world.

Avis, for her part, was already aware of the growing possibilities, and that knowledge was filling her with a sense of anticipation. The future looked like becoming even more brighter than she had ever optimistically expected.

CHAPTER FOUR

The ensuing days were like a dream to Avis. By day she flew into the remotest parts of the area, taking medicines and hope to the lonely people, and during the evenings she enjoyed Duncan's company. Soon it was apparent to her that she was placing more emphasis upon seeing Duncan than upon her work, and this troubled her. Before she had met him her whole life had been wrapped up in nursing and flying, but now she couldn't get her duties over fast enough in order to get back to Kalarra to see Duncan. At times her mind was so filled with thoughts of him that her daily routine was pushed into the background, and several times she found her mind wandering while she was flying. But her job demanded a great deal of concentration, and she was angry with herself for endangering her life and her aircraft by mooning and daydreaming.

In the two weeks until their week-end off together, she and Duncan became very close. It didn't take them long to surmount all the barriers that arise between two people during the initial period of their meeting. Soon it seemed to Avis that she had known him all her life, and she could not imagine what life had been like without him. On his part, he was quite content to be with her, and Avis could see his growing feelings reflected in his face and his eyes when they were together.

With their long week-end upon them, Avis felt happier than she had ever been before. Very early on Saturday morning she and Duncan went to her plane and took off for Perth. Avis was conscious of great happiness as the machine lifted from the ground and soared into the clear blue sky. The sun was powerful, and the brightness all about her was reflected inside her. Duncan was enjoying himself immensely, and one glance at his face informed Avis of the fact. They flew south-west, and there was little talking between them. They were happy enough with their company, and speech was superfluous. When they landed at Perth Mrs Leigh was there to meet them, and Avis felt proud as she introduced Duncan to her mother.

They seemed to get along very well from the start. Duncan was his usual endearing self, Avis noted, and her mother was very interested in him. Avis had never taken home a friend before, and she could tell that this occasion was something of an event for her mother.

Mrs Leigh was tall and slim, very much like an elder sister, if Avis had one. Duncan was quick to remark upon this similarity, and Avis knew her mother was pleased with his words. She smiled as she considered that Duncan should have been a diplomat.

'Father will be busy this week-end despite his efforts to stay free,' Mrs Leigh said. 'He wanted to spend as much time as possible with you, Avis, but you know how hard he works. There's a great deal of expansion going on within the company at the moment and he's at the heart of everything, as usual. But he will be at home tomorrow. When will you have to return to Kalarra?'

'Some time tomorrow afternoon, Mother. But we'll be coming again soon, so don't worry too much. Duncan says he'll make sure I get enough relaxation in future, so you can expect us when our free week-ends correspond.'

'I'm glad to hear that.' Mrs Leigh led the way to her car. 'I've been worried about you, Avis. You work far too hard.'

'I thought the old saying was that hard work never hurt anyone?' Avis queried, with a sparkle in her pale blue eyes.

'Hard work in itself doesn't hurt,' Duncan asserted. 'But the long hours are not so healthy, and the unrelenting tensions. You're going to take it a great deal easier in future, Avis.'

'Yes, Doctor,' she said meekly, and fluttered her eyelids. He smiled at her, and squeezed her hand as they got into the car.

Mrs Leigh drove home, which was a large whitestone house by itself in a select area. Avis looked around with growing happiness, for she loved her home, and she felt a wave of excitement touch her as she planned to show Duncan around. When they got out of the car in front of the house a wave of nostalgia overpowered her, and she had to blink quickly to hold off the tears that came to her eyes.

'This is beautiful,' Duncan remarked as

they entered the house.

'I'm glad you like it,' Mrs Leigh said. 'Avis can show you around shortly. But it's been lonely here without her, I can tell you.'

'Why didn't you get a job in a local hospital?' Duncan asked.

'Because I couldn't fly to and from my work,' Avis retorted, laughing.

'Flying has been my constant rival,' Mrs Leigh said. 'It always had me beaten when I first met your father, Avis. After we were married and you came along I thought I had scored a victory, for if you had been a son I would have lost you to flying. For years I fooled myself with the thought that at least you would be on my side. I knew a son would automatically follow his father. You can imagine my feelings when Avis took to flying, Duncan.'

'I can,' he retorted. 'She lives for it. But I must admit that I'm interested in it myself, and particularly gliding. So I believe the best thing to do if you can't beat them is to join them.'

'I wish I had tried that years ago,' Mrs Leigh said.

'You should have,' Avis retorted. 'If you'd learned to fly you could have visited me at Kalarra, and you'd never have complained of being lonely.'

'It isn't in my blood like it's in yours,' her mother retorted with a smile.

Avis showed Duncan over the house and grounds, and they walked through the gardens hand in hand. He showed enthusiasm for all that he saw, and Avis was happy with his manner. He was genuinely happy to be in her home. It seemed to her that he fitted in without trouble, and she hoped she would find it as easy when they visited his parents in Fremantle, not far away.

'Well?' she demanded when they were standing in the shade of the trees out of sight of the house. 'What do you think of my humble home?'

'Wonderful,' he replied, taking her into his arms. 'I can't understand why you ever left it. You must love flying very much to go look for a job like the one you've got. But I think I can understand something of what moves you, Avis, because I have the same regard for medicine. After all, I left the comparative comforts of Fremantle to go to Kalarra.'

'You did!' Avis nodded, tilting her face to be kissed. 'It would be wonderful if you could become a flying doctor, Duncan, and I was your pilot and nurse. We'd be able to spend our days together as well.'

'Would you like that?' he demanded.

'Very much.' She looked into his eyes and saw something of his own inner feelings showing there. She trembled as his arms tightened about her.

'I think I would do anything for you, Avis,' he said softly. 'But they wouldn't stand for what you suggested. They're finding you too valuable in your present position. But it was a nice thought, and I'll bear in mind that you would like to spend most of your time in my company.'

'That's the way I feel,' she said boldly. 'A girl shouldn't talk like that, should she?'

'It depends what she has in her mind.' He watched her closely, and she saw her reflection in his dark eyes. 'It wouldn't do for either of us to get the wrong idea about the other.'

'What do you mean?' Avis watched him intently.

'I could misconstrue your words,' he said. 'I could place the wrong emphasis upon them.' He sighed heavily. 'I don't know what's coming over me, Avis. You're a pretty strong personality, you know. You overpower me.'

'I do?' She let her surprise sound in her voice, and he took her into his arms and kissed her soundly. 'I haven't made any conscious effort to do anything like that,' she went on when he released her. 'Are you sure it's not your own mind at work?'

'That's quite possible.' There was a teasing note in his voice, and Avis slipped her arm through his and they turned and walked back towards the house. 'We'll talk some more about this, but now isn't the time or the place.'

'You're right. What do you think of my mother, Duncan?'

'She's a wonderful person,' he replied readily. 'I can see how you're going to look as you get older.'

'And does that scare you?'

'No. I think you're going to be very regal in your old age.'

'If I ever live so long!' She smiled as she considered her working days. 'Sometimes I feel as if I shall burn myself out by the time I'm forty-five.'

'You won't do that!' He watched her closely as they strolled towards the house. 'I'm going to take you in hand, my girl, and see that you don't do too much.'

'That will be nice!' She smiled up at him, and there was much in her that needed defining, she discovered. She wanted reasons for the impulses and emotions that swept through her, but to her mind that was impossible. It was fairly obvious that altogether they came under the heading of Love.

That evening they waited for Avis's father to come home, and it was important to her that Duncan should meet him this week-end. But a telephone call later brought a message that he was delayed and couldn't get away. He was flying to Adelaide and wouldn't be back until the next day.

'That's how it is in this family,' Mrs Leigh said, shaking her head in mock sorrow. 'One or another of its members is always absent.'

'Sorry, Mother, but you must be getting used to it now,' Avis said with a little smile, and her mother nodded sadly. 'But Duncan will be coming again, and often,' Avis went on, glancing at him for corroboration, and he smiled and nodded eagerly. 'There will be plenty of opportunities for them to meet.'

'I know, but it isn't right that Father's work should be so difficult to control. At his age he ought to be thinking of taking it easy instead of going on and on like a young man. He's head man in the company, but he works like someone trying to make good.'

'That comes from his conscience and has nothing to do with anything else,' Avis said. 'I'm proud of Father for the way he's worked and built from nothing.'

'And so am I. There's no one more proud,' Mrs Leigh said. 'Yet there is a limit one should give to the world.'

'That's exactly how I feel about Avis,' Duncan said. 'She does far too much.'

'So you two will be allies against me, eh?' Avis demanded. She smiled. 'I didn't bring you here for the week-end just to give you the opportunity of strengthening your action against me. I can see that I've made a tactical mistake. With Mother on your side the odds will be too great. I shall be giving up flying, and probably nursing into the bargain. No doubt I shall be allowed to work a schedule in hospital, going on duty at a certain time and coming off in the same manner!'

'We'll let you do that,' Duncan said with a smile, 'but no overtime.'

Mrs Leigh smiled. 'Tell me, Duncan,' she said. 'How is Avis doing her work? What do they think of her, a winged nurse?'

'They think very highly of her, Mrs Leigh.' He was serious now. 'She's doing a wonderful job, saving half a dozen people from

72

ranging through the bush. She's a flying angel, and don't let her tell you different. There's no praise high enough for her. That isn't my sentiment, mind you. It comes from the top people at the hospital.'

'They always exaggerate,' Avis said, blushing a little. 'I don't want you to get the idea that I'm someone special, Mother. It's far from being the truth. In fact Matron told me a few days ago that I might eventually become redundant.'

'Only because your untiring efforts have helped clean up the area,' Duncan said. 'Doctors were fighting a losing battle out there among the aborigines until you took over, Avis, and you know that.'

'If you tell me enough times then I might begin to believe it,' she replied. 'Don't fill Mother with tales from your imagination, Duncan. I'm just a nurse doing a great job, and I love every minute of it.'

'The fact that you're doing something you like makes all the difference,' her mother said. 'You're very fortunate, Avis, to find your niche in life.'

'I've known that for some time,' Avis said. 'But I'm not satisfied. I think there's a lot more that could be done.'

'Distance makes all that impossible,'

Duncan said. 'I know how you feel, Avis. But your vaccine missions are preparing the way, you know. In ten years, if this present standard is at least maintained, we'll find a great drop in figures of those diseases you're fighting. You'll come out on top because you have the most powerful drugs in the world on your side. When the upper hand has been obtained you'll be able to tell your children, or grandchildren, that you were directly responsible for it happening.'

Avis smiled. She didn't look upon her job in any light other than that it was simple and straightforward, that an aeroplane could cover the distances easily and much faster. There were other medical people in the area doing far more important work, she thought.

Next day she and Duncan went to meet some of her friends, and they had a busy morning, talking to people she knew. It seemed to her that Duncan was enjoying himself, and as they returned to the house for lunch she questioned him about his impressions of the week-end.

'I've thoroughly enjoyed myself,' he said instantly, giving her a searching glance. 'Usually I spend a lonely time when I'm off duty, but all of that seems to be a thing of the past now. I hope you're going to enjoy yourself as much when we visit my parents in Fremantle.'

'I'm sure I shall, because they're your parents,' she retorted. 'But we're almost neighbours, aren't we?'

'Yes, we haven't been living far apart.' He smiled. 'They do say something about gold under one's feet, don't they?'

Avis laughed. Something had been established between them this week-end, she told herself. They had been building up a close relationship upon their off-duty evenings, but this longer period had added something more promising, intangible but obviously there. She could feel it in his glances at her, in her own feelings towards him. It couldn't be explained, but it was there nevertheless.

When they took their leave of her mother that afternoon Avis felt sorry. She would have liked her father to meet Duncan, and knew Duncan had wanted to meet her father, but that could be arranged later without much trouble. But she really felt sorry for her mother, who seemed dispirited despite the fact Avis had been with her that week-end.

'Mother, don't let any of this worry you, please,' she said. 'I know you're lonely, but it's all in a good cause.'

'You may think so, but we have only one life, Avis, and you'll realise that more keenly as the years go by. Father has made his mark in the world, and he doesn't lack money. It's high time he was satisfied with his achievements and learned to live a little. I've waited most of my life for him to get around to doing just that.'

'Do you think a talk might help him see things in a different light?' Avis demanded.

'No, dear.' Mrs Leigh shook her head. 'Your father isn't with us most of the time. His whole life is wrapped up in flying. You know something of what I'm talking, Avis, and you know it better than most because you are his daughter. I've given up trying to change him, but I'm hoping that we'll have some time together, with no interruptions, before one of us dies.'

'Mother, that's a dreadful thought,' Avis said thinly. She frowned as she looked into her mother's eyes. 'I didn't know it was affecting you so badly.'

'It isn't really bad, Avis, so don't think about it yourself. I've got used to it, as a matter of fact. But it was bearable when you were at home.'

'I'm sorry, Mother,' Avis said contritely. 'If I'd known I would never have left home.'

'That wouldn't have been right,' her mother replied. 'You have to go out and make your own way in the world, my dear.'

Avis felt chastened as they took their leave. Duncan shook hands with her mother, promising to see that Avis would return home again in the near future, and Avis kissed her mother's cheek, hugging her as if they would never meet again.

'Goodbye, Mother. I'll ring you each evening in future. But you know I'm always busy, and I never know for certain when I'll get back to the hospital after a day's work. Anything can happen out there in the bush.'

'I know, and that's what I'm afraid of,' Mrs Leigh said, forcing a smile.

'I didn't mean in that respect,' Avis hurried to reassure her. 'There's never any danger. But sometimes I get an unexpected phone call and have to make a diversion to pick up someone, or something.'

'I know how it is, Avis, so don't worry. I'll see you again soon, won't I?'

'Yes. We'll come as soon as we're able.'

'Goodbye, Mrs Leigh. It's been wonderful meeting you. Thank you for having me this week-end.' Duncan was genuine in his words, and Avis felt her heart lift as they walked to her aircraft.

Her mother stood watching until they were airborne, and they dived once to wave. Then Avis set course for Kalarra, and Perth slid away behind them and she wiped all thoughts of it from her mind, although a small, alarming thought of her mother remained in her head.

The flight back was uneventful, and when they reached the hospital airstrip Avis sighed her relief. It was good to be back. An absence of even a few hours made all the difference to her. She could understand her mother's feelings, but knew her mother could never understand either her father or herself when it came to flying. It was more than a pastime or a hobby. It was an obsession, and as such, had to be lived with.

'Avis, this has been a wonderful week-end,' Duncan said as they got out of the plane.

She smiled into his face as she looked up at him.

'I'm so glad you've enjoyed it,' she replied. 'It meant a great deal to me.'

'I felt really sorry for your mother, you know.' His brown eyes were steady as he regarded her. 'You really ought to try and spend more time at home.'

'I'm going to,' she promised. 'I felt sorry,

too. But I can see Father's point of view. Flying is his whole life. If it was taken away from him now he would have nothing. Mother does understand that much about it. But I'm afraid it goes a lot deeper than that.'

'Women have to make allowances when they marry. A man's work must come first, whatever it is. Most women adjust easily, and your mother has done so. But what happens when a couple marry and the wife has an obsession of her own?'

'Then they both have to make allowances,' Avis said promptly.

'That's true.' He watched her for a moment, his eyes keen and searching. 'Would you make allowances, Avis?'

'I haven't considered that part of it,' she admitted slowly. 'My life is so full at the moment I don't get much time for anything else. But with a husband to cope with there would need to be a great deal of adjustment on my part.'

'But do you feel that you could make those adjustments?' he persisted.

'If I married then I would already have made the decision to do so,' she replied.

He nodded, satisfied, and Avis watched his intent face. She had come to know him a great deal better over the week-end. He had seemed different in her home. Out of his usual surroundings, he had appeared as his normal self, his professional side submerged, and she liked the impression he had made upon her. She hoped he had been as favourably impressed by her.

'It's still early,' he said. 'You're not going to leave me now, are you?'

'Not if you don't want me to go.' She smiled. 'But we've been away all week-end, remember, and the plane will need a check–up in readiness for tomorrow.'

'Then I'll help you, if it has to be done now,' he said eagerly. 'I meant what I said to your mother. If I can't beat you then I'll join you.'

'I think we're going to get along very well together,' she remarked with a laugh.

He was as good as his word, rolling up his sleeves to help her carry out the weekly servicing. Avis was happy to have him, although there was little he could do to help. But he wasn't going to stand by and watch. He wanted to learn about the aircraft, and share the work. Avis knew she was going to have a good time teaching him.

By the time they were through the evening was almost gone, and they were both dirty, with oil on their hands and grease on Duncan's white sports shirt. He grinned at her as they cleaned up.

'You're truly an amazing girl,' he said, taking her into his arms and kissing her fervently. 'The more I see of you the better I like you. There never was a girl like you, Avis.'

'Love me, love my plane,' she murmured, her eyes sparkling, and he nodded slowly as he enfolded her tightly in his embrace, holding her as if he would never let her go again. She knew then that their friendship wouldn't remain static. It was going to progress through all the stages to true love, and already she had more than a passing sample of emotion filling her breast. The bright future had never seemed so promising, and all the omens were good. Avis closed her eyes and forgot about everything except the sweet man holding her. She could even give up nursing and flying for him!

CHAPTER FIVE

Monday morning brought her down from her mental clouds, and she reported to the hospital to find two jobs scheduled for her. After supervising the packing of her cases, she was transported out to her plane and given clearance. When she had taken off she felt the old relief billow up inside her, and she smiled to herself as she winged away across the monotonous bushland. She could never forget her good fortune in these first moments of rising into the clear blue sky. Other Sisters were busy in their crowded wards below, but she was free as a bird and the day before her promised to be eventful and filled with rewarding work.

But she did not relax as she sailed through the sky. She knew that people crossed the ground below, and found trouble, and it wouldn't be the first time her sharp eyes had spotted some mishap and saved complete strangers a lot of trouble with a quick radio call to the police. In the back of her mind was the grim scene of the crashed police helicopter. That sort of thing was happening all the time, and one was involved simply because one flew over the territory.

She spotted a black speck in the sky ahead, and tensed a little. Then a smile touched her lips as she sped nearer. She recognised the two-engined plane of Ralph Curtis, and wondered where he was going. Calling him up on her radio, she surprised him, and his good-natured laugh sounded in her ears.

'Hello, Avis, I've been looking for sign of you for the past few days. Our trails don't cross very often. Where are you making for now?'

'Akawoora,' she replied. 'What's on your mind, Ralph?' She was rapidly overhauling him, and as she drew level she throttled down to lose speed. He waved at her, and she replied.

'I'll see you at Akawoora,' he said, 'but it'll be some time before I get there.'

'I'll wait for you. I shall have plenty to do when I get there,' she retorted. 'Goodbye for now.'

She waved again and increased her speed, drawing rapidly away, and the smile was still on her lips as she flew towards the horizon. She liked Ralph, and before Duncan had started taking an interest in her she had felt very attracted to the handsome pilot. But attraction had been all, and she counted upon Ralph Curtis as a friend who shared the same obsession as herself. Ralph lived for his flying. He was unmarried and set in his single ways. He was more at home in the air than upon the ground.

Her thoughts started weaving through her mind, and by the time she reached Akawoora she had sifted every impression gained over the past few weeks. She had a tidy mind, and liked her thoughts to conform, but love and romance seemed to make a girl's mind like a refuse bin. No matter how hard she tried she could not keep a strict control over her thoughts.

Upon landing she set about her duties, having to immunise just over two hundred people. Word of her coming had been passed out a few days previously, and aborigines had been gathering at the clinic ever since daybreak. They were like happy school-children, and Avis knew most of them by sight. They loved her with real devotion, and she had no trouble administering her drugs to them. After carrying out the massive vaccination programme she turned her attention to other diseases, and the children were lined up for examination for trachoma.

Then the feet were examined, and by the time Avis had completed her work she felt tired, and ached in every muscle and joint.

After a meal she forgot about her duties for a moment and went along to the airstrip, seeing Ralph Curtis sitting in the shade of his plane. She had heard his arrival long before, while she had been busy, and she knew he was a busy man with tight schedules. He got to his feet when he saw her, smiling amiably, a medium-sized man with laughing blue eyes.

'I was about to give you up for lost,' he remarked, coming towards her. His pale eyes searched her face closely. 'You look as if you've done three days' work here today, Avis. Why don't they give you an assistant?'

'Probably because I haven't asked for one,' she replied promptly. 'I manage, Ralph. But what's on your mind? You said over the radio that you wanted to talk to me.'

'So I did !' He nodded slowly. 'Come and sit down in the shade for a few moments. You could do with a rest.'

Avis didn't argue with that, and they sat down together under a wing of his plane. She leaned back against the wheel and closed her eyes for a moment.

'They ought to have more imagination,' he

said. 'They ought to know without being told that you can't possibly manage alone. I've a good mind to tell them so myself.'

'Money is short for a service like this,' Avis told him. 'I have to get along the best way I can. I'm doing all right, Ralph. But let's talk about you. What's on your mind?'

'You are!' Their eyes met, and she could see a defiant light in his gaze. 'I felt braver on the radio earlier,' he went on. 'Perhaps I should have mentioned then what was in my mind.'

Avis moistened her lips, but her gaze didn't leave his face. He was very handsome, she thought remotely. She had always been attracted to him. But he wasn't in the same class as Duncan. That was firmly planted in her mind. She was more than halfway in love with Duncan, but could never pass through the attraction stage with Ralph. Her mind felt the shadows of trouble as she divined his next words, and knew she wouldn't be able to avert them in any way. He had evidently been trying to summon up courage to talk to her for quite some time.

'You're not a cowardly man, Ralph,' she said. 'We've known each other for a very long time. We share the same passion.' She glanced up at the large cargo plane. 'We follow near enough the same routine each day. I handle the people's medical needs and you deliver their supplies.'

'I don't want to spoil a beautiful friendship, Avis,' he said huskily. 'But I've been building up about you for a very long time. Now I've reached the ceiling and I'll burst if I don't level out or come down again in a flat glide. The truth of the matter is that I'm in love with you.'

His tones were low pitched and insistent, and Avis felt a sigh gust through her as she stared away into the shimmering distance. There was a brooding silence over the bush, and the heat was heavy and solid, packed in around the plane as if defying it to leave the ground. She looked into Ralph's face, saw the emotions there, and felt dispirited.

'Ralph!' Her voice shook a little, and she was uncertain of what to say, although it was all there in her mind. She had to refuse him firmly, send him back lonely and unsatisfied into the sky of his lonely ways. 'I don't know what to say.' She lost her courage at the last moment. The words were trembling on her tongue but she could not get them past the barrier of her mind.

'You don't have to say anything,' he went on quickly. 'I know this comes as a great surprise to you. We've always been friends, of course, but we've never seen each other off duty, although I'm frequently in Kalarra. Perhaps we can get together in future, some time.' There was an eagerness in his voice which he did not try to conceal, and Avis took a deep breath as she tried to tell him something of what the situation was like.

'I don't want to hurt your feelings, Ralph,' she said slowly. 'To tell you the truth I've always been a little attracted to you. But there is someone else.'

Her voice cut off there and she could say no more. She stared away into the bush, aware that his eyes were upon her. She heard him swallow, and then he stirred at her side.

'I'm sorry for bringing this up,' he said. 'I ought to have guessed that someone like you would have a man in the background. But there was never any evidence of it, and I can't help my feelings, Avis. I would be the happiest man in the world if you could give me something to hope for.'

'I can't.' She spoke reluctantly. 'I wish I could, Ralph.' She looked into his face then, saw the unhappiness that was spreading through him, and sighed heavily. 'Only a few weeks ago I might have felt something,' she floundered. 'But what's happened to me came about quite suddenly.'

'They say a faint heart never won a fair lady,' he retorted. 'So that's what's beaten me, eh?' He laughed harshly. 'I've been toying with the idea of talking to you for weeks. If I'd done so when I first thought of it I might have clicked.' He shook his head. 'I suppose it wasn't meant to be! Well, that's how it goes.' He reached out and took her browned hand between his own small, strong hands. 'Don't let this come between us, Avis. We can still be friends, can't we? I always get a good feeling when I see you.'

'It won't make any difference to me, Ralph. I always look forward to seeing you. I just hope that you won't feel too hurt by what I've said.'

'Forget about it. I spoke out of turn, anyway. I ought to have been more subtle about it.' He laughed, but there was a forced note in the sound of it. 'I've still got my flying. At least we share that enthusiasm, Avis.'

'We do,' she agreed. 'It's the greatest thing in my life.'

'And mine.' He glanced at his watch, then sighed. 'I've got to be moving. I'm late as it is.'

'That's for waiting for me,' she said.

'Well, I don't mind waiting around for you. Where are you making for next?'

'Bush Mission!' She got to her feet and stretched wearily. 'But I haven't so much to do there. Then it's back to Kalarra.'

'I'll see you around. I'm going north now. Got a couple of drops yet to do. So long, Avis. I'm glad I spoke to you despite my failure. I feel better inside with the uncertainty gone.'

'I'm sorry you failed,' she told him gently. 'I really am.'

'I know.' He grinned and held her hands for a moment. 'You'd better get away first. Are you all ready to go?'

'Yes. Goodbye, Ralph.'

He walked with her to her plane, and stepped back when she was ready to take off. They waved to each other and then Avis departed, raising dust as she travelled faster and faster across the bumpy airstrip. Once airborne, she circled, very low, and waved to Ralph again, and then she swept away and settled herself to going on to the next stop; Bush Mission, a hundred and fifty miles to the south-east. Her thoughts were sombre as she concentrated upon her flying.

It was strange how one formed an attachment for one particular person and felt nothing for anyone else! But a few weeks ago she might have fallen in love with Ralph if he had shown a personal interest in her. But he had always treated her as a fellow aviator, a friend who shared the same overruling passion. She hadn't even guessed at the emotions building up in him. Now she was sorry for him, because he would feel the loss of her friendship keenly, as she would miss his cheery character. There would have to be some changes in their relationship, no matter how either of them felt. She would always be conscious of the fact that he loved her, and he wouldn't be able to forget that he had told her and had failed to interest her.

She sighed silently as she flew on. The loneliness was a great comfort and she was thankful that she didn't work in a hospital. Out here, aloft and alone, her business was her own and not subject to the gossip and interference that occurred all too frequently among the nursing staff of any large hospital. She was thankful that she was an individualist.

At Bush Mission she put down the plane on a small strip and bumped towards the main building. There was a large group of children waiting outside the clinic building, and she smiled as her personal thoughts went into the background of her mind. She alighted from the aircraft and locked it, chocking the nose wheel before walking off.

This was the great part of her job. She could visit settlements many miles apart and treat patients with little or no trouble. It didn't matter that the bush was hostile by its vast being. She could flit here and there like a moth, delivering drugs and medicines that formed the main attack against disease, and the figures were already showing great promise. This method of fighting illness was successful. Preventive medicine was a great thing. It wiped out the widespread effects of disease, and cut down the attention needed later by more skilled medical people. This was a two-fold action Avis was fighting, and she was aware of it. The knowledge was the only thing that sustained her during moments of great weariness and strain.

She had been at the Bush Mission only three weeks before, with the vaccine that fought poliomyelitis. Now she was back to check the children again for trachoma.

It was a constant fight against all the diseases that plagued the aborigines. Nothing was ever overlooked, and results proved the value of her work.

But she was worried as she worked. Ralph Curtis was a good man and deserved to find happiness in life. He was in love with her, but she was not available. It was as simple as that, and yet she could not help feeling responsible for her failure to help him. The fact that she was falling in love with Duncan didn't seem to help. Ralph had fallen in love with her. The knowledge did something to her inside that showed no tangible effects. But she felt altered in some way, as if a tiny part of her mind had been cut out and the resulting void had been filled with numbness.

Before she left Bush Mission a telephone call from the hospital reached her, and she went in answer. It was Matron's office, asking her to call at a settlement and pick up an injured man on her way back to Kalarra. She could reach the man long before a helicopter. Avis acknowledged the message and recorded the details. Then she took off and flew to the settlement.

Hers was a varying job, although the routine work that came of her was visiting the many aborigine settlements. She even flew sacks of mail to the various settlements if she was going in a particular direction and her course corresponded. Sick passengers were frequent, and she returned former patients to their homes if they lived in remote parts of the area. Nothing came amiss. Medical supplies for the various permanent stations always travelled with her, and she was a welcome visitor wherever she touched down.

The injured man needed specialist attention, and he was helped gently into the plane. Avis took off with him, handling the controls as gently as possible, and she was concerned all the way back to Kalarra. Ten minutes before she arrived she radioed her position, and when the airstrip came into view she saw an ambulance waiting. She landed perfectly and taxied in, and after the patient had been removed from the cabin she sighed a little and relaxed.

Now that her day's work was over she had the feeling that it had lasted far longer than the many hours she had spent on duty.

There was a longing to see Duncan deep inside her, and she knew she had been disturbed by Ralph Curtis and his declaration of love. She went into the hospital and visited the Matron's office, getting details of her next day's work schedules, then she looked for Duncan, and found him in his office.

'Avis. I was hoping you'd get in early,' he

said. 'Are you feeling too tired for an evening out? I've been invited to a party, and I'm sure it's just the thing for you. I don't think you get enough diversion these days. Have you got a best dress you can slip into?'

'Certainly.' She smiled. 'A party sounds just what the doctor ordered.'

'Good. I'm glad that you agree.' He studied her face for a moment. 'I'm inclined to talk to the medical authorities about you,' he remarked. 'I'm sure that job is too much for you. Why don't you ask for an assistant? You have quite enough to do flying that plane, Avis.'

'But I'm a nurse first and a pilot second,' she retorted with a smile. 'I'm all right, Duncan, really. Don't worry about me.'

'If I don't worry about you then no one will,' he said. 'I don't like to see you looking so tired when you come in after a day's duty. I'll speak to Matron when I get the chance.'

Avis smiled, but made no reply. There was a picture of Ralph Curtis in her mind, and she was wondering why his declaration of love should upset her so. It wasn't as if she didn't know her own mind. She didn't have to make any choice between two men. But she could feel the sorrow that must be living in Ralph's mind now, and she didn't like to think that she was responsible for it.

'I'll pick you up at seven-thirty, Avis,' Duncan said. 'I think that will give you time to have a nap. You should do that, you know.'

'I'll think about it,' she replied. 'But before I clean up I'll have to check the plane.'

'That ought to be done by a mechanic,' he retorted. 'Really, Avis, the way you're treated is shocking. You're a maid of all work.'

'I like it like that, Duncan. Don't worry about it.'

He shook his head slowly and got to his feet, coming around the desk to stand before her. There was a bright expression in his brown eyes, and Avis felt a surging rush of emotion going through her. She was in love with him! The knowledge was alive and bright inside her. Some of her low spirits fled before the knowledge, and she closed her eyes thankfully as he took her briefly in his arms. His kiss reassured her and filled her with happiness. She felt more her old self as he released her and showed her to the door.

'I don't want to get rid of you,' he said in apology. 'But if I'm to get out of here at six-thirty then I've got to get a move on.'

'I'm not the only one who's busy,' she retorted as she took her leave. 'Why don't you try to get an assistant, Duncan?'

He smiled and shook his head. 'See you later, sweetheart,' he said.

'I'll be ready at seven-thirty,' she promised.

Her tiredness returned more strongly after she had serviced the plane and satisfied herself that it would carry her without trouble through the next day. She went to her quarters in the Home and fought against the desire to sit down for a moment. If she succumbed to the temptation she would never get ready for the evening. She showered, and that helped to chase much of her weariness away. Then she sat down and relaxed, and her eyes closed and she slept until a hammering at the door awakened her.

Alert as soon as she opened her eyes, Avis glanced at her watch as she got to her feet, and she was amazed to see the time was almost seven-thirty. Someone was still banging at the door, and she smoothed her dressing gown and patted her hair as she went in answer. A Sister told her Duncan was waiting.

'Would you tell him to give me ten minutes?' Avis said, and the woman nodded and smiled as she went away.

Avis was flustered as she finished dressing, and by the time she left the room the hands of her watch were pointing out a quarter to eight. She was breathless as she hurried out of the building, and Duncan came smiling from his car to greet her.

'Don't tell me; you fell asleep earlier and my arrival awakened you,' he said.

'That's exactly what happened,' she replied, smiling ruefully. 'It's a good thing I had got nearly ready before I sat down.'

'Well, it's a sign that you are doing too much,' he warned sternly. 'I'm serious about talking to Matron about this.'

'I don't think you'll get much joy.' Avis shook her head. 'The hospital is short of nurses as it is.'

'Your work is every bit as important,' he decided. 'But let's forget about the hospital for this evening. We've both put in a great deal of time today, and we need to forget about it if only for a few hours.'

Avis agreed, and they got into his car and drove off.

'Where is this party being held?' she demanded.

'It's a medical do, I'm afraid, so there will be a certain amount of shop talked. Merrick Ramsey is giving the party. He has two or three a year, you know.'

'I do know, but I've never been to one of

them before. I was asked to the last one, but found something else to do that seemed more important at the time.'

'But this time you haven't been able to do that.' He smiled. 'Unless you feel that going out with me is the more important thing.'

'Perhaps that's it,' she conceded with a smile.

'Am I at all important to you?'

'Now you're fishing. What do you want me to say?'

'That I am the most important man in the world for you.'

'You're the most important man in the world for me,' she said gravely.

'But do you mean it?' He glanced at her for a moment, then returned his attention to the road.

'I wouldn't have said it if I hadn't meant it.' She spoke seriously, her brow furrowed as she considered Ralph Curtis and his words that day. Poor Ralph! But she couldn't love two men, and it was better Ralph found out the truth without waiting for it. He would be able to forget her sooner by knowing his chances.

'You seem subdued,' he observed slowly. 'Are you still feeling tired, Avis?'

'A little,' she admitted.

'Then we won't stay late at the party. We'll just put in a social appearance.'

'I don't want to spoil your fun, Duncan. We'll stay as long as you like.'

He reached out a hand and patted her shoulder. 'There's never been another girl like you, Avis,' he said firmly. 'I'm one of the luckiest men in the world.'

'I hope you'll never have to regret getting to know me,' she returned hesitantly.

'Never!' he vowed. 'No matter what happens, I'll never feel that way about you or your memory.'

She smiled, feeling a little easier at his words. She was only just beginning to realise that romance was not the simple boy loves girl routine that she thought it was. A person's feelings were all caught up, and terrible pain could be caused by a thoughtless action or word. It went much deeper, to the very heart and root of life itself, and she made a vow that she would never treat anyone's feelings lightly, ever again...

CHAPTER SIX

Doctor Merrick Ramsey lived in a large house on the outskirts of town in the fashionable quarter that had slowly built up away from the more bustling sections of business and commerce and industry. More than a dozen cars were already in the great park beside the house, and Avis frowned as Duncan parked and they alighted. She imagined they were in for an evening of shop talk, and she didn't feel inclined for that sort of thing on this particular evening. But Duncan seemed keen to attend, and she made no protest for his sake.

Entering the house, they were immediately met by Mrs Ramsey, a tall brunette nearing forty, and there was an apologetic smile on her still-glamorous face.

'I'm so sorry, but Merrick has been called out on an emergency,' she said. 'But perhaps he won't be long. Do come in. I'm sure you know everyone present.'

'Hello, Eve,' Duncan greeted. 'Have you met Avis Leigh before?'

'We haven't met,' Eve Ramsey said, smiling and holding out a hand to Avis. 'But I've heard a great deal about you, Avis. You're very welcome here. My husband is an ardent admirer of your method of nursing. You've saved him a great deal of travelling in the time you've been operating out of Kalarra.'

'I'm glad someone has benefited from my work,' Avis replied with a smile. 'It justifies my existence.'

'But we don't want to talk shop tonight,' Duncan said. 'I'm certain Avis is being overworked, Eve, and if I do get the chance to say a few words in the right ear this evening I'm going to take it.'

'Don't, Duncan,' Avis begged, and Mrs Ramsey smiled and turned to meet her next guest.

'Help yourself to a drink inside the lounge, Duncan,' she said. 'I'm sure you know everyone here.'

'Thank you, Eve, don't worry about us,' he replied.

Avis felt a tightening of her expression as they went into the spacious lounge. There was a large crowd present, and a quick glance at the assembled faces showed her that she did know most of them. Several of the Sisters from the hospital were there, and so was Phyllis Anson, the matron. Of the men present, Avis recognised two or three doctors, and they all stared with interest at her and Duncan.

Miss Anson came forward as Duncan left Avis to fetch drinks. She greeted Avis warmly.

'I was hoping you would come, Avis,' she said. 'Do you think I might fly with you tomorrow?'

'There'll be room, as far as I know,' Avis replied. 'Is there something special about tomorrow's schedules?'

'It isn't that.' There was a gentle smile on her superior's face. 'I have the day off, and I'm utterly sick of following the same old routines. I promise not to make myself a nuisance if you will let me fly with you.'

'I shall be very glad of your company, Matron,' Avis told her. 'But I leave very early in the morning.'

'I know. I always feel a trifle guilty when I think of the long hours you put in, Avis. I'm sure you do too much alone. I often look at you when you return, and you always seem worn out.'

'Then you'd better not mention the subject to Duncan,' Avis retorted with a smile. 'He's got a bee in his bonnet at the moment about that. In fact he's going to make the opportunity this evening of bringing it up.'

'Could you do with some help then?' Miss Anson's dark eyes were filled with query. 'I know you get more than enough to do, but so do most of the nursing staff. However, your work is more tiring, and you work many more hours than a normal Sister. If you think you should have an assistant then I'll be only too happy to consider the fact and do what I can to appoint someone.'

'There are times when I could do with an extra pair of hands,' Avis admitted slowly.

'It must be too much for you if you're prepared to admit as much,' came the quick, firm reply. 'All right, Avis, I'll see what I can do. Tomorrow I shall be able to get some idea of what your routine entails, although I have been out with you before and seen what you get done. We mustn't have you overworking. You have to fly your plane as well as attend to all those people. You'd be surprised at the number of glowing reports that come in about you, and from some most unusual people.'

'I'm sure most of them are blinded by the fact that I pilot myself around,' Avis said.

'The work itself is nothing out of the ordinary.'

'I won't have that,' Miss Anson said stoutly. 'I've seen the way you work and I know.'

Duncan returned with two glasses of sherry, and his eyes lit up when he saw the Matron.

'Good evening, Miss Anson,' he said. 'I was hoping you would be here this evening.'

'Good evening, Doctor Ross. I was just talking to Avis about her work. I have the feeling she could do with an assistant, don't you?'

Avis laughed at the expression which came to Duncan's face, and he glanced quickly at her, his eyes widening. He opened his mouth to speak, then closed it again, and Miss Anson laughed girlishly.

'I'm going out with Avis tomorrow, purely in an unofficial capacity, you understand, and if I see that she does need help then I shall have a trained nurse assigned to her duties.'

'That's more like it,' Duncan said, nodding firmly. He grinned at Avis, and she felt a wave of warm emotion sweep through her. 'How did this subject come up, anyway? I thought we weren't going to talk shop this evening!'

'It's one of the most difficult things to avoid doing in our business,' Matron said. 'We don't merely perform a duty, we live the part.'

Avis agreed with that, and nodded her approval. Duncan shook his head slowly, and there was a harshness about his face which she had never seen before.

'They expect too much,' he said.

'The medical authorities?' Miss Anson demanded, and he nodded. 'I sometimes think you're right, but from what I've seen in my experience it is the only way they can approach the business. It is totally different, won't you agree, to any other business in the world?'

'We're dealing in people and their infirmities,' Duncan agreed. 'But there's very little difference in the business management, surely. I think too much is placed upon the fact that we deal in people and not motor cars. Look at a garage. A mechanic is a car doctor, broadly speaking. Yet we are bound hand and foot and he is not.'

'And we won't talk shop this evening,' Avis said with a smile.

'Sorry.' Duncan drained his glass and held out his hand for Avis's. But she declined. 'I'll get another drink then,' he said. 'Can I get something for you, Matron?'

'No thank you. I believe in keeping spirits for medicinal purposes.' She laughed lightly, and Duncan excused himself. When he had gone Miss Anson regarded Avis with steady brown eyes. 'Duncan is a fine man and an extremely good doctor, Avis. How do you find him? You two have been keeping company for some weeks now, haven't you?'

'Yes.' Avis stared after Duncan's tall figure with loving eyes. 'We've become very friendly lately. Neither of us has made a habit of running around in our free time. But we seem to get along quite well together.' Her softly spoken words gave no hint of the feelings she had for Duncan, and her tones were quite unemotional. But Miss Anson was watching her with that sharp glance of hers, and Avis had the feeling that despite her casual attitude to the question, Matron knew perfectly well what was going on in her mind.

'I thought, at one time, that he wasn't quite human,' Matron said. 'He didn't show the slightest interest in women at any time, except a professional interest in his female patients. But I've seen him change during the past few weeks, and we have you to thank for that, Avis. You've changed, too, even if you don't realise it.'

'Not for the worse,' Avis said with a smile, and added: 'I hope!'

'Certainly not. You're a dedicated nurse, but you were too intense about the whole business. Since meeting Duncan you've changed, become more aware that there are other things in life than just nursing. That's a good thing, Avis, and I hope you'll continue to make progress.'

Duncan returned, and Miss Anson went on to speak with some of the other guests.

'Merrick has just returned,' he said, 'and he's got a chap named Curtis with him, who wants to see you, Avis.'

'Ralph Curtis?' Avis started nervously, for her mind had been working subconsciously on thoughts of Ralph and his declaration of love for her.

'That's the chap. He was at the hospital asking your whereabouts when Merrick returned there.'

'Where is he now?' There was a frown on Avis's face as she looked towards the door.

'He's waiting in the study. That's about the quietest place in the house right now.'

'Then I'd better go and find out what he wants. Will you excuse me, Duncan?'

'Certainly.' He smiled as she started away

from him, but Avis could see a questioning light in his dark eyes.

She left the room and saw Ralph standing in the doorway of the study, talking with Merrick Ramsey, who turned with a smile at her approach.

'Hello, Avis,' Ramsey said, a tall, heavily built man with a permanently worried face. 'I've saved this friend of yours a bit of trouble. You can use the study to talk.'

'Thank you, Merrick.' Avis looked into Ralph's face. 'Is something wrong, Ralph?' she demanded.

'I'm sorry to trouble you like this, Avis,' he replied. 'But it is urgent.'

'Let's go into the study,' Avis told him, and he stepped out of the doorway to permit her entrance. Then he followed her and closed the door. 'What's the trouble?' she demanded.

'My plane conked out at Broken Ridge Mission on my last trip of the day,' Ralph said. 'It's nothing serious, and I'll be able to fix it in fifteen minutes. But I can't get out to it unless I waste half a day tomorrow. I was wondering if you would fly me up there when you take off tomorrow.'

'I'll be glad to, Ralph,' she replied instantly. 'You know we're always ready to help one another in cases like that.' Then she paused. 'But I've promised Matron a trip with me tomorrow. She likes to get out now and again to look around the missions and settlements.' She sighed. 'I can't get both of you in the plane at the same time.'

'Oh.' He pulled a face. 'Well, forget about me and I'll have to wait until I can get a lift. One of the farmers promised to pick me up if I couldn't go along with you.'

'But you wouldn't get out to Broken Ridge until well into the afternoon if you travelled by ground transport,' Avis said. 'I know you're as busy in the area as I am, Ralph. Would you care to fly out now?'

'I did have that in mind,' he said hesitantly, but grinning. 'But I can't drag you away from this good party. You don't enjoy yourself half enough. I'll bet this is the first party you've attended in the last couple of years.'

'That's true.' Avis shrugged her shoulders. 'But there will be other parties, Ralph. If you want to get out to Broken Ridge then I'll fly you out now.'

'My company will pay the price of your petrol,' he said. 'They are anxious for me to get back as early as tomorrow morning. I have a big day ahead of me.'

'It will take about two hours to fly to

Broken Ridge,' Avis mused. 'I could get back to the party at about the time it breaks up.'

'No, Avis.' Ralph shook his head emphatically. 'I can't drag you away from all this. You deserve a break. You go on and enjoy yourself.'

'Do you think I would be able to, knowing you're in trouble?' she demanded. 'Don't say another word, Ralph. I'll fly you out there tonight. Just give me a couple of minutes to explain the situation to Duncan.'

'He's the boyfriend, huh?' Ralph demanded. His pale eyes glinted as he searched Avis's face. 'I am sorry about this,' he said again.

She smiled and turned to the door. 'I won't be long,' she said. 'I expect Duncan will drive us to the airstrip. You haven't got a car here, have you?'

'No.' He shook his head. 'I'm a damned nuisance, aren't I?'

'These things can't be helped,' she replied. 'I won't be long.'

Finding Duncan, she explained the situation to him, and saw his face record disappointment. But he shrugged fatalistically.

'I was half expecting something to come

along and ruin the evening,' he said. 'Either I would be called out or someone would want you. But don't worry about it. My only concern is for you. Four hours' flying now will have you pretty tired in the morning. It wouldn't have been so bad if he'd turned up earlier.'

'But it took him a long time to get in from Broken Ridge,' Avis pointed out. 'If he waits until tomorrow to get back he'll lose a day's time. He's as busy as I am, delivering supplies to the various settlements.'

'It's government work. You'd think he could commandeer a police helicopter, or something.'

'I know. I don't like the idea of turning out, but Ralph wouldn't hesitate to help me if I were in trouble.'

'Of course. Do you want me to drive you to the airstrip?' There was a gentle smile on Duncan's face, and Avis nodded slowly.

'If you would. Merrick brought Ralph here, and he hasn't got a car. The sooner we start out the sooner we'll be back.'

'Is there a chance that I can accompany you?' Duncan demanded.

'No.' Avis shook her head. 'I'm sorry. I'd love nothing better than to have you along, but there's not enough room.'

His face showed his disappointment, and he sighed. 'All right, I'll come back here after you've gone, and then pick you up again later. It'll be a good four hours, won't it?'

'At least four hours,' she replied. 'But before I go I'd better have a word with Matron. She wants to go with me tomorrow. I may not get the chance to see her again tonight.'

'Perhaps I'll be able to fly with you on my day off!' Duncan sounded hopeful, and she paused in the act of leaving his side.

'I'd love that! It did pass through my mind, but you have to relax too, Duncan, and it's no picnic spending the day with me.'

'Don't you believe it,' he retorted. 'I'd put up with every kind of discomfort for that privilege.'

'Then we'll talk about it later.' Avis was smiling as she sought out Miss Anson, and she quickly explained the situation to the Matron.

'I'm sorry you've got to go, but I'll keep an eye on Duncan for you,' came the swift reply. 'Sister Gilbert has always been sweet on Duncan.'

'I didn't know that.' Avis glanced around the room, and her pale blue eyes glinted as they came to rest upon the slender figure of Valerie Gilbert, a tall, glamorous brunette. 'Perhaps I ought to try and squeeze Duncan in the plane after all!'

'Don't you worry about him!' Miss Anson smiled as she patted Avis's shoulder. 'I'll be at the airstrip at seven sharp. That's when you'll be taking off, isn't it?'

'At seven,' Avis confirmed.

'Well, don't worry about anything. I shall help you all I can tomorrow.'

Avis smiled as she left, and Duncan followed her into the hall, where she introduced him to Ralph. She could sense them sizing up each other, and a frown touched her forehead as they went out to the car. She sat in front with Duncan, and Ralph sat in the back. They were silent for the most part on the drive through town, but Ralph did lean forward and apologise for the trouble he was causing.

'Don't apologise,' Avis told him. 'You'd do as much for me if I were in similar trouble. I can remember when you did fly me back to town once.'

'That was different,' Ralph said thinly. 'You're working on the medical side of taking care of the natives. Your work is very important.'

'And yours isn't?' She half turned to look into his intent face. 'What would happen if your supplies didn't get through?'

'All right.' He laughed. 'I'll take your word for it.'

'But I do feel that they should make adequate arrangements for emergencies like this,' Duncan said thinly, concentrating upon his driving. Avis could see that his wide shoulders were stiff, and there seemed to be resentment in his whole attitude. She frowned as she considered the cause for his feelings. Of course he would be disappointed that their evening out together was ruined, and he was concerned that she wouldn't have much rest before having to face another stiff day tomorrow. But her instincts told her it went deeper than that, and a little thread of worry pulled tight in her mind.

'I've been telling my bosses the same thing for years,' Ralph said. 'But they operate on a shoestring, you know. You can't get blood out of a stone.'

Avis sat in silence until they reached the airstrip, and while Ralph fetched his spare part for his plane from the hospital entrance, where he had left it, she contacted flight control and gave them details of her trip. Confirmation came through and she switched off the radio and climbed out of the little cabin. Duncan stood in the shadows, waiting for her.

'Will you be all right flying through the darkness?' he demanded anxiously.

'Of course!' She smiled. 'I have instruments.'

'It's all rather beyond me,' he retorted. 'Perhaps we can start flying lessons for me. I want to understand all that you do, Avis.'

'Any time you like,' she told him.

'I'm going to worry about you until you get back,' he went on, glancing at his watch. 'Can you go any faster?'

'It will take four hours, there and back,' she said.

'What about fuel? You're all ready for take-off tomorrow, aren't you?'

'I can check over the plane again when I get back.'

'This chap Curtis. Have you known him long?'

'Ever since I've been operating from here. We often cross each other's trail in the sky, and sometimes I see him on the ground when we're at the same mission or settlement.'

A car approached, its headlights glaring, and when it pulled up beside them Ralph

Curtis alighted with a long parcel under his arm.

'All ready?' he demanded.

'All ready,' Avis confirmed.

'Good. I don't want to keep you away longer than necessary.' Ralph looked into Duncan's shadowed face. 'I appreciate the way you've taken this, Doctor. Not every man would have been so polite about another man taking away his girl, and from a good party, too.'

'It's all in the cause for humanity,' Duncan said steadily. 'I'm used to making sacrifices in the cause of medicine, and Avis is the kind of girl who must do what she can, regardless of time or trouble. It's one of the things I really admire her for.'

'Well, we'll be getting on our way.' Ralph started climbing into the plane. 'I hope we'll meet again, Doctor. I've been curious about the kind of man who can interest Avis. I never thought she would meet someone who could take her mind off nursing even for a moment. I was most surprised when I heard about you.'

Duncan said nothing, and Avis slipped into his arms for a moment. He kissed her lightly. 'I shall be waiting impatiently for your return,' he said softly. 'Take care, Avis.'

'I'll be all right,' she told him. 'Thank you for being so understanding about this, Duncan.'

He squeezed her arm and she turned away, climbing into the cockpit and closing the door. She saw Duncan step back, a tall, shapeless figure in the shadows, and she shattered the silence with the powerful roar of the engine. She had felt sad at the thought of spoiling the evening with this trip, but now she was at the controls and ready to take off she felt relieved that she didn't have to stay at the crowded party.

She wondered at herself in those few moments of racing along the strip, gaining flying speed. Surely there was something abnormal about her! Normal girls liked parties and social contact, but she was only really happy when she was flying through the air on a nursing mission. Her work meant everything to her, and it seemed that even her growing love for Duncan took a back seat when duty called.

They became airborne, and she looked down at the ground as she realised that she hadn't thought to circle and wave farewell to Duncan. A frown touched her brows as she set course for distant Broken Ridge, and the lightness inside her contained nothing of the disappointment she ought to have felt at having to leave the man she loved.

A small doubt became apparent in her mind, and it took root despite all her efforts to dislodge it. She tried to prevent it getting a hold of her frontal mind, but it loomed horribly, and she had to face it, drag it out into the open and look at it as if it were some surgical specimen. Did she really love Duncan or was the prospect of finding romance blinding her to real emotion? Could it be that she was falling in love with the thought of falling in love? Had she donned rose-coloured spectacles for the first time in her life?

She didn't know! And she didn't like the questions or the doubts. Hers was a very realistic life, and despite her great many hours spent in the air she knew she had to keep one foot firmly upon the ground, if only in her mind.

CHAPTER SEVEN

The two-hour flight was uneventful, and Avis and Ralph didn't converse much. She let her thoughts hold sway, and her doubts did not recede as she considered them. Was she making a mistake? That was the main thought in her brain. But she didn't know the answer. She couldn't begin to find the answer. She realised that she needed more time. Perhaps she was trying to hurry herself into love because she was afraid of missing it altogether. Her mind had seized upon the situation with Duncan as if there were no other men in the world who might show an interest in her. She glanced into the surrounding darkness, and caught sight of Ralph's reflection on the perspex. He was behind her, peering across her slim shoulder, and she sighed as she considered what he had said about his feelings for her. They were both lonely people, and seemed to be two of a kind. She couldn't help wondering if she would fit into Duncan's world. But she would certainly know where she was with Ralph.

It came to her that Duncan had seemed perfectly at home at the party, but it had bored her, despite the fact she knew all the people present. She had come to rely upon her own company for pleasure, and although being in love meant making some sacrifices, she wondered if she would be strong enough to give up all she loved. There would be little room in her future for flying or nursing if she married Duncan.

'Not far now, Avis,' Ralph said in her ear, and she started out of her thoughts and glanced at the clock. Checking her course and the instruments, she nodded.

'Another twenty minutes. I'd better call them up.'

'I telephoned from the hospital at Kalarra to tell them to expect us,' he said. 'You're a great girl, Avis. There aren't many who would give up a precious evening for me.'

'I wasn't too happy at the party, Ralph,' she admitted. 'So don't let it worry you.'

'Okay, I won't. I had the feeling you were relieved to get out of there. But I must say Doctor Ross seems a very nice person.'

'Thank you, Ralph. He is one of the best.'

'He's a very lucky man. He doesn't know how much I envy him. I hope you'll be very happy with him, Avis.'

'We haven't got that far, Ralph, so you'd better save your congratulations until the event takes place.'

'You mean there's a chance that he isn't the right man after all?' There was a note of eagerness in his tones. 'Have you been thinking over what I said to you?'

'No, Ralph.' She spoke in low-pitched tones that were barely audible above the note of the engine. 'I don't think any man is right for me. I feel out of it somehow, and it's difficult to explain. I'm doing the job I was born for, and I don't think there's any room in my life for anyone else.'

'Don't say that.' Enthusiasm sounded in his voice. 'I'll bet I can make you change your mind.'

'Don't try, Ralph. Please don't try,' she said.

They were silent until the few landing lights at the strip came into view. In a matter of moments they had touched down and taxied in, and Avis sighed deeply as she switched off and climbed out. Ralph followed her to the ground, and he carried his spare part.

'Avis, you're an angel,' he declared. 'I would have wasted a complete day tomorrow if you hadn't gone to all this trouble.'

'It was my pleasure, Ralph,' she replied.

'Really? Do you mean you would rather had flown me out here than attended that party?'

'That's the way I feel right now.'

He dropped his package with a resounding thud, and the next moment Avis was in his arms. His mouth came hard against hers, and she was surprised at his strength, and so astounded that she could not struggle. She let him kiss her, but did not respond, and when he realised that he slowly released her.

'I'm sorry. I shouldn't have done that, I know. But I've been crazy about you for months, as I told you. If you're not serious about Doctor Ross then perhaps you can come to love me in time, Avis. We're two of a kind, you know. We like the same things, and we are lonely people. I know we'd get along well together.'

She made no reply, but her emotions were suffering a great upheaval. There was a picture of Duncan in her mind, and a dull kind of knowledge was informing her that they would never be able to find happiness together.

'Ralph, I don't know whether I'm coming or going right now,' she told him tremulously.

'I'm sorry. I guess I let my feelings run

away with me. But I do want you to know that I think you're the most wonderful girl in the world, Avis. I can't explain how much I care about you. My admiration defies all bounds. I'd give my right arm to share your life and your future.'

She looked into his shadowed face. A cool breeze blew into her face, ruffling her hair. The starlight gave them both a tinge of unreality. She shivered involuntarily, nerves taut, instincts flaring. She tingled as if a shock had passed through her from some giant generator. Emotions which she could not begin to understand came to life in her breast.

'Ralph, I've always admired you,' she said in low tones. 'I don't want you to get me wrong. I like you. But I don't think I'm capable of loving any man. I have my work, and that seems to occupy the whole of my life.'

'I think I understand, but does Doctor Ross?' He shook his head slowly. 'I have the same stresses inside me, Avis. I know what makes you tick. That's why I think I could make you happy.'

'I don't think love could ever make me happy,' she said slowly. 'I live for my work and my flying. That's more than enough for me.'

'The last thing I want to do is cause you any worry.' He stood too close to her, and she could feel a tugging sensation in her breast that caused her uneasiness. He had always attracted her, and now she realised it. But she wasn't in love with anyone. She knew that with a dull ache coming to life with the knowledge. Duncan was important to her, but seemingly only as a friend. She didn't know the meaning of love, unless it was love for what she was doing and not for some person.

'I'd better go,' she said hesitantly. 'I have a long way back, and in the morning I've got to be at the hospital airstrip at six.'

'Avis, if there's ever any way I can repay you for this then you've only got to mention it,' he said firmly. 'You'll let me have a bill for the petrol you used tonight, and your time, won't you?'

'We'll talk about it the next time we meet,' she said. A sigh escaped her. 'Shall I wait around until you see if you can fly again?'

'No, don't bother. I've troubled you enough already. You get back, and be careful. I don't want anything to happen to you. You're too wonderful to be taking risks, anyway.'

'If you had your way I'd be wrapped up in

cotton wool,' she told him, and he nodded vigorously.

'That's exactly how I do feel about you. You've hit the nail right on the head.'

Avis turned away slowly, feeling reluctant to start the two hours' flying back to Kalarra, but thought of the next day was uppermost in her mind, and she smiled at him as she stepped back on to the wing of her plane.

'I'll see you around, Ralph,' she said softly.

'Thanks again, Avis, and happy landings!'

She nodded and got into the cabin. She felt stifled as she taxied along the strip, then turned into the wind. The landing lights were flickering and she blinked as tiredness drifted across the face of her mind. Then she breathed deeply and took off, swinging around in a wide circle to pick up her invisible course. There was a strange sensation in her mind that embraced Ralph and Duncan, and indecision ached inside her. If this was love, she thought remotely, then it was far better to remain outside its deadly pressures and worries. Until she had started falling for Duncan she had been the happiest girl in the world, without a care to trouble her, but now she felt five years older and prey to every fear under the sky.

On the long flight home she imagined she

would be able to sort out her problems, but her mind was giddy with working around in a circle. Nothing straightened out in her mind. It was like being on a merry-go-round. The sensations were exhilarating but the effects were disconcerting. When she reached Kalarra and landed, Duncan came forward. His tall figure stood erect before her, and Avis felt her emotions twist and swell.

'You're back safe,' he said, taking her into his arms, and when he kissed her there was a picture of Ralph in her mind.

'I'm tired,' she said dully, 'and I have to be up very early in the morning.'

'I wish there was something I could do to help, but you're in such a unique position that no one can do anything for you.' His tones betrayed his worry, and she tried to relax in his arms. But she could feel the strength of Ralph's arms about her, and she shivered as she tried to rid her mind of the impression Ralph had made upon her.

'I must get out of here before six in the morning,' she said. 'I did have the plane ready, but it will have to wait until morning now. I can't do anything more tonight.'

'I'll take you home. Have you locked up?'

She nodded, bracing herself erect. Her

shoulders felt like sagging and her legs trembled. She had never felt so tired before, and knew her mental condition was aggravating her physical state. She walked with him to his car and sank thankfully into the seat. Duncan tut-tutted as he got behind the wheel.

'Avis, I'm going to keep a strict eye upon your activities in future,' he said firmly. 'Your doing far too much. I'm a doctor and can see it clearly. I won't have you knocking yourself out in this way. Something is going to give inside you if you don't let up.'

'The way I feel right now, I'm inclined to agree with you,' she said slowly.

'I don't want anything to happen to you,' he went on, starting the car and driving from the strip. 'You're too precious to me.'

She studied his profile as they travelled the short distance to the Nurses' Home. He was precious to her, she realised, and a little warmth travelled through her. Duncan was becoming part of her life, despite the indecision and doubt in her mind. The fact that Ralph was able to move her emotionally just proved that she was trying to hurry herself into love. If she stood back and took a deep breath, and tried to be patient, everything would work out right. Of that she was sure!

For a few moments she was actually happy again, and felt that her troubles were over. But when Duncan parked outside the Home and took her gently into his arms she again found a large picture of Ralph Curtis before her mental eye. It was most disconcerting to find the real pleasure gone from Duncan's lips, and her imagination thrust up sensations that had gripped her while in Ralph's arms instead of giving her memories of the pleasure received from being kissed by Duncan. She put it down to over-tiredness, and was thankful when Duncan didn't keep her. He kissed her gently, then released her.

'You hurry in now, Avis, and get to bed as soon as you can,' he told her. 'You must take it easy. I don't know what I'd do if anything happened to you.'

She took her leave of him and went in to her quarters. It was almost too much trouble for her to get undressed and take a shower, but she did so, and then climbed thankfully into bed. Her eyes closed before her head touched the pillow, but even with the light out she could not relax and drift into sleep. Her mind denied her the luxury, and she sighed and turned impatiently. But her exhaustion fought against her mind, and slowly she sank into blessed unconsciousness...

It seemed that her mind had hardly relaxed before the alarm clock was ringing, and Avis blinked when she opened her eyes, aware of great tiredness. She reached out a wavering hand and turned off the alarm, then sat up, rubbing her eyes, stifling a yawn. A glance at the hands of the clock had her throwing off the bed covers, and she pulled on a dressing gown and started her morning routine.

At a little after six she was at the airstrip, checking over the plane, looking forward to the day's work. When she was satisfied that all was ready she went into the hospital and collected her cases and bags for the day. She usually carried a large supply of vaccine, drugs, tablets and sundry medical supplies, and this morning Miss Anson was travelling with her. By the time she was ready for take-off the time was almost seven, and she sat down under the wing of the plane and waited for Matron.

Miss Anson arrived only a few minutes after seven, dressed in a gaily patterned dress, looking nothing like a hospital matron. She stifled a yawn as Avis got up to greet her.

'Sorry if I've kept you waiting, Avis. I expect you've been up a long time, haven't you?'

'About a quarter past five,' Avis admitted, and she saw Miss Anson wince.

'And you had four hours of flying last night. What time did you get to bed?'

'Around midnight. Will you get in first?' Avis helped her superior into the close cabin, then got into her seat. She closed the canopy and went through her checklist before calling the air control staff to report she was ready for take-off. The airstrip was not very busy, especially at this time of the morning, and a cheery voice wished her happy landings and gave her permission to take-off.

Miss Anson was silent until they were airborne and flying towards their first destination. Then she leaned forward to speak in Avis's ear.

'You missed a wonderful party last night, Avis. It was a great pity you had to leave.'

'I must confess that I was relieved to get away,' Avis told her. 'I'm not really cut out for that sort of thing.'

'You need to relax now and again. That's professional advice, although you'll be aware of that from your own experience. You are working too hard, Avis, and despite the shortage of trained nurses, I'm going to assign someone to help you.'

'It may not work out, Matron. Sometimes I have to bring in a sick patient, and there isn't room for three in the cabin. If I had to leave my assistant somewhere while I brought in a patient it would mean flying all the way back to pick her up again.'

'We'll go over it later,' Miss Anson promised. 'There must be something we can do to alleviate the pressures.'

Avis was happy with Matron's company. She felt she needed to talk to someone, and although Miss Anson was her superior there was no gulf between them that rank usually brings to hospital staff. One could always talk to Miss Anson as one would talk to a confessor. But what was in Avis's mind was not in a fit state to be broached as a subject. She felt overwhelmed with tension, and anticipation throbbed in her breast for all her attempts to forget her personal life. Yet it wasn't thoughts of Duncan that bothered her but the prominence that Ralph had achieved, first by his declaration of love for her and then with his kiss the previous night.

She felt her lips burn as she remembered the incident. A series of pictures fluttered through her mind, showing her past incidents involving Ralph, and she knew he had been firmly embedded in her life as a casual friend who loved the same pursuit that crazed her. It was strange to think of him in a different light, in the age-old way a woman thought about a man. Then there was Duncan. He held a special place in her life. She was half in love with him, or had been until her doubts became too strong for her wavering emotions. Now she didn't know if she loved him or not.

'Duncan is rather sweet, Avis. He moped around the party last night after you left, just wishing away the time until he could come and meet you. I think you've made a conquest there, and you're a very lucky girl. He's a man in a hundred! A lot of the nurses would give anything to be in your shoes.' Miss Anson paused for a moment. 'I think I'm a little envious of you. Sometimes I think of you up here, when I'm busy at the hospital, and I'd give anything myself to swap places.'

'It isn't all flying, Matron.' Avis smiled as she checked her course.

'I'm the first to realise that, Avis. I know I work you very hard. But in future the flying ambulance will have to turn out to save you the trouble of bringing in a sick patient. I know you carry a lot of unofficial stuff for all kinds of people. I don't intend putting my foot down about that, but you're to have an assistant, and nothing must stand in the way of that.'

'Did Duncan have anything more to say on that subject after I left last night?' Avis demanded.

'We talked of nothing else. I'm so pleased that you two nice people have got together that I'm willing to do anything to help. But apart from that I'm convinced that we've given you too much to handle in a day. Other nurses have regular hours of duty, and so should you. I'm thankful to Duncan for bringing this matter to notice. You would never mention it in a thousand years. You're that kind of a girl. But I'm not one to flog a willing horse, Avis, and you must have an easier time of it.'

'This morning I feel as if I could do with an easier time,' Avis admitted.

'You never take regular time off,' Miss Anson went on. 'I don't want to talk an ear off you, Avis, but you're going to have some free time in future.'

Avis nodded. On this morning of all mornings she was ready to listen to advice.

She squinted her eyes as she stared down at the ground, watching the shadow of the plane speeding on before them across the rough, desolate terrain. Soon they would be arriving at a settlement. She called up on her radio and gave details of her position and estimated time of arrival. Then she returned her attention to Miss Anson.

'I'll help you today, Avis. Class me as your assistant, and tomorrow you'll have a nurse with you. I've put a notice on the staff board, asking for volunteers to work with you, and when we get back today we can look over the candidates together. You can pick anyone you think will prove a help to you. Is that all right?'

'It sounds fine, Matron,' Avis said with a smile. 'But I shall feel a fraud, taking a nurse away from her full-time duties.'

'We've got to take care of you! You're most important. The work you are doing is vital, and you would be irreplaceable. I just can't take any risks with you.'

Avis felt warmth fill her at her superior's words. So she was really justifying her existence! It made her feel good to have evidence of that. All the hard work and the wearying days made her wonder sometimes if she was having any good effect, and Miss

Anson was telling her she was.

The bright sunlight glared in her eyes, and she frowned a little when the airstrip came in sight. There was the usual crowd of natives waiting to see her land, and Avis looked for the windsock to check the direction of the wind. When she touched down on the bumpy strip she was conscious of great pleasure. Now her personal thoughts were gone into the background and her professional self was preparing to go to work.

Miss Anson proved to be a great help, taking care of the children while Avis checked her lists and handed out the vaccine doses. In what was a remarkably short time they had completed the treatments and carried out the routine medical checks. Over a cup of coffee Miss Anson discussed the help she had been.

'How much time have you saved, Avis?' she demanded.

'A good hour and a half! I usually get done here around lunch. But now I can get on to the next stop, and when we've finished there we should be able to reach Kalarra about four-thirty.'

'And you started out at seven, to say nothing of the time you spent servicing the plane before you could take-off.' Miss Anson shook her head. 'It's still a lot of hours, Avis. Far too many for you to maintain the routine day after day without a break.'

'An assistant will be enough help, Matron,' Avis said with a smile. 'I don't mind the long hours.'

'Perhaps we should cut down the number of your calls. If you made one visit a day that would help. You'd be back in Kalarra by noon, or just after, each day, and you've not got to spend each evening servicing your plane. It could be done in the afternoon.'

'You want me to work only half days?' Surprise sounded in Avis's voice, and Miss Anson smiled.

'One visit a day would still see you doing eight hours and more. You're not supposed to work any harder than that. All the nurses work an eight-hour day, Avis, and you shouldn't be any exception. If anything, you should work less hours, because you have more strain in this work than an ordinary nurse on a hospital ward.'

'It's going to take me some time to get used to the idea.' Avis shook her head slowly. 'I shall feel as if I'm not doing anything at all. And if I cut down to just one trip a day I'm not going to get around to all the places I have to visit.'

'If you go on at your present rate then in a very short time you're not going to visit any place. You're working yourself into the ground, Avis, and it's got to stop. The sooner you get that idea firmly fixed in your mind the better you'll be able to adjust your new working regulations.'

'Duncan has really started something, hasn't he?' Avis didn't know whether to be pleased or sad. 'Before long we'll have another nurse and plane on the rounds.'

'And that might not be a bad idea at that,' Sister Anson told her. 'I was waiting for you to reach that observation, Avis. If at any time you go sick, or are unable to complete a day's work, we're going to find ourselves in a spot of trouble. The regular flying medical services would have to take over, and that might disrupt quite a lot of schedules and treatments. We've got to look after you, my girl, and I intend making the effort to start that business right away.'

Avis didn't feel like arguing. There was relief inside her, for now that it had been pointed out to her she could see that she had been working too hard, trying to cover too much ground. The area of her rounds was something in the region of three hundred thousand square miles, most of it remote and tough bushland. The climate didn't help her at all, and although she would never have made a protest on her own behalf she was thankful that Duncan had the good sense to see that she needed help.

Duncan! Her mind conjured up a picture of him. She felt a little guilty when she recalled the previous evening. She had run out on him, using Ralph as an excuse. She had acted selfishly because she hadn't felt comfortable at the party. But if she had any love for Duncan at all she would have acted unselfishly, would have thought of his needs first. That was what troubled her. She had always considered herself to be unselfish. Time and trouble didn't enter into her scheme of things when she was doing some-one a favour. But since her first feelings of love for Duncan had come into being she had felt subtle changes taking place. At times even her valued work had taken second place in her thoughts, and that was near sacrilege.

Could all these little changes be a direct result of her own changing attitude? It was possible, and she disliked change most intensely. But love was not without problems, and she would have to face up to that fact if she wanted romance and love like any normal girl...

CHAPTER EIGHT

It was early by her normal standards when they reached Kalarra again, after covering the day's schedule, and Avis sighed with relief when she and Miss Anson stepped out of the hot cabin on to the strip. Miss Anson stretched and smiled, shaking her head slowly.

'I don't know how you do it every day, Avis,' she said. 'I don't mind the trip now and again, but I will say that it's a bit too much for a regular routine. But what have you to do now?'

'Just check over the plane, return the cases to the hospital and pick up tomorrow's schedule,' Avis said.

'And help me select your assistant. The car is coming now. Leave everything here for the time being and we'll attend to the administration first. I want you to get settled with someone you can work with. After that we'll see how things go.'

'All right.' Avis nodded, conscious of relief. The car arrived and she put her cases inside. There was a sigh upon her lips as she got in beside the driver and Miss Anson sat in the back. When they reached the hospital she felt some of the load shifting from her shoulders, and she was content to let Miss Anson take the lead when they reached the matron's office.

There were three applicants for the job of being Avis's assistant, and Miss Anson called them into her office one at a time. The matron asked a series of questions destined to get to the bottom of each application, and Avis sat silently by, content to accept anyone who seemed keen enough for the job in hand. She agreed with Miss Anson's decision that Nurse Eden would be suitable. Avis liked the girl's instant replies to some of the more difficult questions, and the girl's interested face proclaimed that enthusiasm for flying was partly responsible for her application.

'I must warn you, Nurse Eden, that Sister Leigh puts in some very long hours in the course of a day. I accompanied her today, and I'm not sorry to be back, I can tell you.'

'I'm not afraid of hard work, Matron,' Nurse Eden said, her blue eyes glinting. 'I've always admired Sister Leigh, and I'm sure she won't be able to find anything wrong with my work.'

'All right, Nurse. I'll leave you to Sister Leigh's tender mercies. She'll tell you all about the job, and when you'll be leaving tomorrow. Are you off duty now?'

'Yes, Matron.' The girl was barely twenty-three, tall, slender and beautiful, with steady blue eyes that were almost as pale as Avis's.

'Come and have a talk with me then, Nurse,' Avis said, getting to her feet. 'I have to go back to the plane now, so you can look it over.'

'I shall be happy to,' the girl said, and they left the office together.

Avis paused in the doorway. 'I'll look in later for tomorrow's schedule, Miss Anson,' she said.

'It will be ready in about an hour,' came the smooth reply. 'I trust you'll find your duties much easier after this, Avis.'

'Thank you,' Avis replied. 'I'm sure there'll be no more worries about the way I work or what I have to do.'

She was relieved as she and Nurse Eden went back to the airstrip. She took the opportunity to study her new assistant, and she liked what she saw. Nurse Eden seemed capable, and there was an air of enthusiasm about her that made Avis like her even more.

'Have you ever done any flying, Nurse?' she asked.

'Once,' came the swift reply. 'A boy friend took me up. I loved it. I can't wait to get up there again.'

'You'll probably get sick of it by the time you're settled with me,' Avis said with a smile. 'Either you like flying or you don't. If you like it you won't care about the hours or the heat, but if you don't take to it then you'll never find a more horrible way of travelling.' She paused, glancing at the girl. 'What's your name, anyway? I'm not going to call you "Nurse" all day long, and I don't expect you to call me "Sister".'

'I'm Estelle Eden.'

'And I'm Avis Leigh.' Avis was smiling. 'I'm sure we'll get along all right, Estelle. It's pretty much of a routine, and it won't take you long to get into the way of it. No doubt you know what my work consists of.'

'Yes. I have heard. You fly around all the settlements, attending to all the natives.'

'That's about the sum total of it. But there's an almighty lot of flying to do, and many, many hot hours cooped up under that canopy.'

They were approaching the silent plane now, and Avis could see the admiration and

143

excitement in Estelle's pretty face. She smiled, remembering her own early days of flying, when most of the art had still been a mystery to her. She could understand something of this girl's thoughts.

'It seems so small,' Estelle said, her pale eyes glinting.

'It's quite safe,' Avis replied, smiling. 'With regular servicing there's very little danger of any trouble while you're up there. Engine failure is another thing, and quite in the lap of the gods. But it isn't something you want to dwell on.'

'I'm not afraid.' Nurse Eden was breathless with anticipation. 'What time do we start out in the morning?'

'I usually take off at around seven. With two of us to handle the treatment I think we can put it on half an hour. We'll go at seven-thirty. I haven't got the schedule yet for tomorrow, but it won't be more than two visits. I had Matron with me today, and she helped. I finished well ahead of time.'

'I'm so glad I was chosen. I promise you'll never have cause to rue this, Avis.'

'We'll get along all right together,' Avis said, glancing at her watch. 'Come on, I am a bit early. Let's go up and fly around for half an hour. It will be better for you to find out now if you're suited to the job than to wait until tomorrow, when it would be too late for me to turn back.'

Estelle was all for it, and they climbed into the cabin and Avis prepared for take-off. Once aloft, she set course for the bush, and gave her new assistant an acrobatic flight that was designed to test her ability to fly. Estelle came through the test with sparkling eyes and a wide smile, and Avis was satisfied as they dropped down to the hospital air-strip. She made a perfect landing and taxied to a small hangar.

'Well?' she demanded as they alighted. 'What did you think of it?'

'Words fail me,' the girl said. 'It won't seem like work to me, Avis. I wish it were morning already.'

'Steady on,' Avis said, laughing. 'I've just finished a long stint. I want a good night's rest before I have to start out again tomorrow. Now I've got to go over the engine. You run along if you want to, Estelle, and I'll see you here about seven-fifteen in the morning.'

'I'd like to stay and watch what you do,' the girl said eagerly. 'If I may I'd like to learn as much about flying as possible. Will you teach me?'

'If you're that interested then of course I will, and be only too pleased to have someone to share it with. But I promise you will get heartily sick of flying before another month has passed.'

'I don't think I will, but if I do then I'll tell you. Is there anything I can do to help you now?'

'No. Don't dirty your hands when there's no need. I won't be long. See you in the morning, Estelle, and don't wear your uniform. It'll be stifling in the cabin most of the time. You can see what I wear when I'm working, and I advise you to do likewise.'

'This job gets better and better the more I learn about it,' Estelle said with a laugh. She took her leave, and Avis watched her critically, liking the girl in the first instant, and knowing that they would be able to work together.

By the time she had finished servicing the plane, Avis was tired. She had been in the sun too long, and wanted nothing more than a lazy shower. She could imagine the cool water beating against her skin, and hurried up to get finished. It wasn't until she was near the hospital that she thought of Duncan, and a frown creased her brows. For the first time since Ralph had kissed her she had forgotten her doubts and problems. She smiled. So that was how serious it all was! At the first sign of mental occupation all her worries fled!

She went into the hospital, aware that she was grubby, but she had a reputation around here of not being a conformist, and people expected to see her with oil on her hands and specks of dirt or smears of grease on her face. She went to Duncan's office and tapped at the door, and his deep-throated invitation to enter filled her with longing. She entered the office and stood before him. He was at his desk, writing up some reports, but he put down the pen and sighed and got to his feet when he saw her.

'Avis! I'm glad to see you back. I've been thinking about you all day. How did it go?'

'Not too badly at all. Miss Anson helped me like a trained assistant all day.'

'And you're having an assistant from now on,' he said.

'Yes. I've just selected her. Nurse Eden.'

'That pretty little blonde! I know her. She's a keen type. I'm glad she got the job. She should be a great asset, Avis.'

'I've taken a liking to her,' Avis admitted.

'And you're not too tired? You had a heavy day yesterday.'

She smiled, pleased by his concern. 'I'm not too tired,' she told him. 'I am, after all, as strong as a young horse.'

'But those long hours every day can pull down the strongest and fittest. But I think we've caught you in time. Can we go out this evening? Nothing strenuous, I promise you. Just a drive and some company.'

'I'd like that,' she told him gently. 'I spoiled your evening last night. I'm very sorry about that, Duncan.'

'No matter.' He waved a cheerful hand. 'Life is all a matter of priorities, and I recognised last night that your fellow aviator had more need of you than I.'

'Ralph is a good sort,' she said, and wondered why she had to defend him. She was aware that Duncan was watching her closely, but there was a smile upon his face. 'We have to help each other whenever possible, as I explained last night. I never know when I may need his help. It's a long way home from some of those settlements.'

'I know that, Avis, so don't try to explain anything to me. I liked the look of Curtis myself. He's just the type for that work he does, and I should imagine he's quite capable in any sort of situation.'

She nodded, feeling easier in her mind.

She glanced down at herself, seeing the stains from servicing the plane, and she smiled. He laughed as he caught her glance, and read what was passing through her mind.

'You look awfully sweet,' he said, putting his arms around her shoulders. 'Avis, I love you. I can't keep it to myself. I want to tell you and everyone I know. Am I being a fool?'

'Of course not.' She looked steadily into his eyes, and there was a gentle smile on her face. 'We've known each other for a long time, although it's only recently that we've been seeing each other. But I like you. That much must be obvious from the fact that I like being in your company.'

'You do?' He bent and brushed his lips against her cheek. 'I have been hoping to hear that from you. I won't expect more than that at this time. I'm not going to be impatient, but I want you to know that I'm not just filling in my time with you, Avis.'

'I'm glad to hear that!' She smiled, pushing herself into his arms, tilting her face to be kissed, and he held her tightly, kissing her with controlled passion, and starting her mind off with wonderful thoughts. All her doubts had really gone! She wondered if she had been worrying subconsciously about her work, and that it had been the cause for her doubts. Now the threat of overworking had been removed she was feeling normal once more. Ralph didn't seem to matter now, and she was relieved that she could be firm with that in mind. She was in love with Duncan, and time itself would prove it to her and everyone else.

'Avis, let's try and make it a long evening together,' he said, stroking her hair. 'Hurry home and get cleaned up. Take a short rest, but let me meet you early.'

'Where are you going to take me?' Her eyes showed her agreement, and he kissed her gently.

'Where would you like to go? Do you feel like dressing up and taking in a night club? I'd like to see you in those glossy surroundings. I was beginning to enjoy myself at the party last evening, but you were taken from me.'

'That would be nice,' she replied without hesitation. It was in her mind that she had spoiled the evening for him, and she had accused herself that very day of being selfish. She had to make allowances for his likes and dislikes, and if she loved him then conforming to his wishes would be all part of the magic of loving him.

'All right.' He showed his pleasure in the brightness of his brown eyes. 'I'll call for you at about seven-thirty. That will give you plenty of time to get ready, and have a rest before doing so. You're not looking so tired today, and most of the strain has gone from your face.'

'Miss Anson saw for herself today how much I have to do,' she told him. 'That's why the new assistant has been appointed. But it will seem strange working with someone. I've led a lonely life, and I think that's the part of it I've really enjoyed.'

'Never mind about that. Humans weren't meant to be lonely.' He kissed the tip of her nose. 'Now run along and let me get these reports up to date. See you later, Avis.'

She smiled and departed, and there was the old familiar lightness inside her again. Going to the Nurses' Home, she took the shower, then relaxed in her room. There was a feeling of great satisfaction inside her, and it stemmed from her relief. Everything was going along fine again.

At seven-thirty she was ready to go out, and watched from a window for the first sign of Duncan. He drove up in his large car and she waved to him from the window before grabbing up her handbag and hurrying from the room. He was waiting at the door for her when she reached the ground floor.

'You look a picture,' he told her, smiling gently. 'I've never seen a more beautiful girl, Avis. No wonder I was attracted to you. There's not a nurse on the entire hospital staff who can compare with you.'

'Thank you, kind sir!' she retorted. 'You certainly know how to flatter a girl!'

'You're looking more refreshed now, Avis. Did you have a good rest?'

'Yes, Doctor!' she smiled as their glances met. 'I carried out your orders.'

'You make a very good patient. But I hope I never have to treat you professionally.'

'Any time I'm ill I'll take care of myself,' she retorted.

'Don't be so independent, Avis!' There was mild reproof in his tones. 'Other people like doing things, remember. You get a great kick out of helping people, so why don't you give others a chance to do some helping once in a while?'

'Sorry, but there is a strong family trait running through my character. The Leighs are very independent.'

'I've already discovered that,' he retorted

with a smile. 'But tell me, have you rung your mother yet?'

'My mother?' She shook her head. 'I haven't found the time.'

'Naughty!' He shook his head slowly as he helped her into the car. 'You promised you would call her each evening.'

'I'll do it later.'

'Not this evening! By the time you get back here it will be long past bed-time.'

'Are you keeping me out late?' she queried, smiling.

'No, because you're going to get some early nights in future,' he replied.

'That doesn't sound so good.' She shook her head.

'Doctor's orders!' He was smiling gently, but there was an expression of determination on his handsome face, and she nodded slowly.

'I'll do whatever you say, Doctor.' She could not prevent a wave of emotion from sweeping up inside to engulf her. A longing for love caught her unguarded, and the pain in her breast was as real as any physical twinge. She watched him walk around the car to the driving seat, and as he slid in beside her she put a hand on his shoulder. He looked at her quickly, an eyebrow rising in query.

'Something wrong?' he demanded.

'Nothing wrong. I want to be kissed,' she said simply.

'Here, with half the nursing staff watching from their windows?'

'I don't mind. But don't do it if you're afraid your reputation will suffer.' There was a teasing note in her voice, and he laughed as he recognised it. 'I'll spoil your make-up if I kiss you,' he warned.

'I can repair it as you're driving,' she replied.

'Then no further discussion is necessary.' He took her into his arms with boyish eagerness, and Avis closed her eyes as he kissed her. 'That better?' he demanded as he released her.

'Much better!' She leaned back in her seat with a satisfied expression on her face. 'You'll have to do that more often, Duncan.'

'You're different this evening,' he observed, shaking his head slowly. 'What's come over you?'

'How am I different?' she wanted to know.

'It's something I can't put my finger on.' He frowned as he started the car and drove away. 'You were not like this last night when we went to the party.'

'Perhaps I was over-tired,' she suggested, her eyes darkening as she recalled all her doubtful thoughts of the past twenty-four hours. 'But I'm all right now, and there's no time like the present, Duncan.'

'Hooray for the present!' he commented drily. 'I hope it will never end.'

Avis really enjoyed the evening. She could understand his observation that she had changed, for she felt it keenly herself. Something had lifted from her mind and it wasn't the fact that she now had an assistant to take care of part of the work. Work had never worried her to that extent. It had made her very tired, but she had always been happy doing it. She knew it was something else, something more personal, and it was too new and fresh in her mind for any explanation to be forthcoming.

Duncan took her into the most fashionable club in Kalarra. It was nothing to be compared with the more expensive establishments in Perth or Fremantle, but by Kalarra standards it was the last word in luxury and entertainment. Dinner was a cosy affair, and Avis did full justice to the meal. Duncan chose a light wine that tasted like nectar, and glints of happiness beamed in Avis's blue eyes as she relaxed and enjoyed herself.

There was a cabaret, and the entertainment was good. She hadn't enjoyed herself so much for a long time, and the knowledge that she had been missing a great deal by keeping her nose to the grindstone added to her enjoyment now.

'No need to ask if you're happy, Avis,' Duncan said, leaning across the table and covering one of her brown hands with a larger, gentle hand. 'We're going to do this sort of thing more often, my girl.'

'I am happy, Duncan,' she whispered. 'Thank you for taking trouble with me. I must be a most difficult person to accompany. Do you think the rough edges on me can be smoothed?'

'There are no rough edges,' he responded gallantly. 'You are different, and that's all. I appreciate your attitude to life. You're like a wild thing that's trying to domesticate itself, but instinctive fears are at work inside you, unsettling you and preventing complete understanding. But persevere, Avis, and it will all come right in the end.'

'Do you want me domesticated, as you called it?' she demanded.

'I don't know.' He shook his head slowly. 'I'm afraid the process may rob you of something precious. You stand out in a group,

Avis. There's some undefinable quality about you that sets you apart. Perhaps it is your way of life, that irrepressible sense of freedom, but it's greatly apparent, and I wouldn't want that sheen dulled for anything. Promise me you won't change. Say you'll always be as you are now.'

'I'll do my best,' she said gently. 'But everyone changes in life, Duncan.'

'In some ways,' he agreed. 'But I don't think you can change, Avis. I hope not, anyway.'

They danced on the small floor, and it was heavenly to be in his arms and seeming to float in time to the music. Avis felt all her first optimistic sensations of love rising unchecked inside her. It was wonderful to feel so relaxed and happy! But her happiness wouldn't have been so complete if Duncan hadn't been with her. He made everything perfect, and she was happy with the knowledge. Now she could laugh at all her previous fears and doubts. She had been trying to force the pace, and that accounted for the onset of worry. Realisation of that fact alone brought a remedy, and she was perfectly content now.

But as they returned to their table she caught sight of a well-known face, and her heart seemed to miss a beat when she recognised Ralph Curtis. He was in the company of another man, and he was coming straight towards their table. Avis caught her breath as Duncan held her chair for her. She suppressed a sigh, telling herself that she was being foolish by admitting, even by manner, that Ralph had some effect upon her. Duncan was the man she was in love with, and she hoped that anyone with a practised eye could tell the fact, truthfully and completely. But she was aware of a curious pounding sensation in her throat as Ralph paused by her side, and when he spoke she saw Duncan look up with surprise, then glance at her quickly with a small, tell-tale expression that seemed to say he felt something in the atmosphere around Ralph.

Avis forced a smile she was suddenly far from feeling. Duncan was aware that she had been placed under pressure by Ralph, and the knowledge hurt her. She didn't want to cause him a moment's worry. But she was equally certain that Ralph meant nothing to her in the deepest sense. For a few hours she had imagined he did, but that was safely behind her now. She sought for some way of letting Duncan know, but a glance at his intent face told her that he was fighting a mental battle of his own, and she was slowly and surely pushed into a defensive attitude. Yet the knowledge that Duncan was feeling the first pangs of jealousy did something to her. It strengthened her confidence in herself and straightened her crooked thinking. She was on the threshold of discovering exactly what it was she wanted from life, and the facts were in the hands of these two handsome men.

CHAPTER NINE

'I'm not interrupting anything, am I?' Ralph demanded, pulling up a chair and seating himself at Avis's side.

'Not at all,' Duncan said immediately. 'I'm always pleased to see a friend of Avis's.' He glanced at the man who was accompanying Ralph. 'Does your friend want to sit down?' he invited.

'I'd like to introduce him first,' Ralph said. 'He's very anxious to meet you, Avis. He wants to get to the Sweetwater settlement. I know you were in the area a few days ago, but will you be going back again very soon?'

'I shan't be able to take passengers again, Ralph,' Avis told him slowly. 'I have an assistant, starting from tomorrow, and she'll be with me at all times.'

'That's a bit of a blow.' Ralph watched her intently, his blue eyes gleaming in his weathered face. 'What happens if I ever need a lift?'

'I'm sorry but I won't be able to help you,' she said.

'I see.' He was thoughtful for a moment, then he shook his head. 'I don't like the sound of that. Whose idea was it that you have an assistant?'

'Mine, in the first place,' Duncan said coolly. 'Avis has been working far too hard and long, and I set the wheels in motion.'

'But you very often carry patients to and from hospital,' Ralph persisted. 'What about them?'

'All the details have been taken care of.' There was a note in Duncan's voice that gave Avis the idea that he was enjoying this, and she watched him closely. But his face was expressionless. 'In the past Avis has been taken too much for granted. She's always been willing to do whatever she can to help people, and they have accepted her

160

regardless of the effort it cost her. In future she won't be used so much.'

'Are you beginning to feel the pace?' Ralph demanded, subjecting her to a close scrutiny.

'A little,' she confessed. 'But the job itself has grown since I started, and in a year or so I expect there will be another plane in operation. I'm sorry I can't help your friend, Ralph, but it is rather out of my hands now.'

'I understand.' He nodded. 'I shan't bother to bring him over then.' He paused and seemed to consider for a moment. 'Do you think you could possibly run him out to Sweetwater when you've finished your work one day?' he demanded.

'I forbid that,' Duncan said in surprisingly strong tones. 'Last night was almost too much for her. She can't say no, and I am saying it for her. What about your plane, Mr Curtis? Don't you fly in that direction?'

'I'm more tightly bound by rules and regulations than Avis,' Ralph said, shaking his head. 'Otherwise I wouldn't have bothered her. It may surprise you to know, Doctor, but I have a great deal of feeling for Avis, and I care what might happen to her. She and I are of the same kind. She understands, and so do I. I don't think you do.'

'That is as may be.' Duncan was cool and calm, but determined. 'But I do have Avis's interests at heart, and I'm a doctor. I know what I'm talking about. She is on the verge of breaking down.' His eyes met hers across the table. 'That's a clinical fact,' he said, nodding. 'Even you didn't realise it, Avis, but all the signs were there. That's why Matron acted as quickly as she did. That's why I'm trying to impose my way on you, Avis.'

'I have been feeling peculiar lately,' she admitted, and recalled her frightening thoughts of the past twenty-four hours. 'Thinking of it, Duncan, I feel sure you're quite right. I've been working myself to a standstill.'

'I'm glad you're at last aware of it.' Relief showed in his face. He sighed as he faced Ralph again. 'So there's your answer. Avis cannot do any extra flying.'

'I agree with you,' Ralph said readily. 'I wouldn't want anything to happen to her. I'll tell my friend he'll have to do it the hard way. His business is important to him, but no one is going to fall sick if he doesn't get there, or go hungry. I guess you are the most important one among us, Avis.' He smiled. 'Now excuse me and I'll go. I'm sorry I interrupted your evening.'

Avis remained silent as he got to his feet, and he looked down at her for a moment. She could feel Duncan's eyes upon her and heat touched her cheeks.

'I'm sorry I can't help you, Ralph,' she said. 'I would if I could, you know that.'

'I know.' He patted her shoulder. 'Don't worry about it. I'll see you around. So long.'

He nodded at Duncan and turned away, and Avis watched him going back to his friend. She heard Duncan sigh, and when she looked at him he was watching her.

'I'm sorry if I took what seemed an unreasonable line, Avis,' he said. 'But you have been taken too much for granted, and it's about time that sort of thing was stopped.'

'That's all right,' she said eagerly. 'You're the doctor, you know. I've been a good nurse, and I promise to be a good patient.'

'Does Curtis mean anything at all to you?' he asked slowly.

Avis regarded him for a moment, thinking over his words. Then she shook her head. 'Not in the way you mean,' she said. 'He's a very good friend, as I've already told you. But he's no more than that!'

'I think you mean a great deal more to

him,' Duncan said tensely.

'I know.' She watched his face steadily.

'Any man would be a fool if he didn't have some feelings for you,' he grunted. 'If he is in love with you then I feel sorry for him. I know what it is to love you.'

'You're very sweet and understanding, Duncan.' She reached out and touched his hand, and he allowed a smile to soften his harsh features. 'I'm so very glad I met you.'

'Are you?' He nodded slowly. 'You don't think I'm dictatorial?'

'If you are then it's only for my own good,' she retorted. 'Can I quarrel with that?'

'Avis, I wish a couple of months would pass in a flash,' he said with great enthusiasm.

'Why?'

'Then I'd be more sure of you! This is a very difficult affair I'm trying to conduct. You're so busy and so am I, and there seem to be so many diversions.'

'Don't worry,' she assured him. 'As far as I'm concerned there's only one man in this world.'

'And that is?' he persisted.

'You,' she told him shortly.

They danced again, and although Avis relished their contact something seemed to have vanished from their mood. She found herself looking around for sight of Ralph, but he must have left immediately, and there was a picture of him in her mind as Duncan checked the time and then decided it was too late for them to stay longer.

On the drive back to the Nurses' Home, Avis leaned in her seat with her head resting lightly against Duncan's shoulder. From time to time he reached across and stroked her hair, and she held his hand tightly, as if his strength would help her retain the better feelings she held. She seemed on the brink of losing something valuable, but didn't know what. It was like a premonition, and it scared her. But she showed nothing of her concern as they said goodnight. Duncan kissed her gently, and then she went in to bed.

The alarm clock did not fail her next morning, and she sighed wearily as she sat up to switch it off. For a few moments she sat staring around the room, collecting her thoughts and gathering herself for the start of the day. Then she remembered that her assistant would be with her, and she smiled and got out of bed.

She was down at the airstrip just after six, and by the time Estelle Eden arrived, about a quarter past seven, the plane was ready for take-off. They went into the hospital to collect the drugs and medicines, and Avis was filled with relief when they were back at the aircraft and preparing to take-off.

Estelle was trembling with excitement when they were in the cabin, and Avis took the time to speak with the girl before calling the local flight controller and reporting her destinations and time of departure. She received the daily weather forecast, and learned that a storm was expected in the area. But she had plenty of experience in local storms, and took off rapidly.

'How do you like it, Estelle?' she called over her shoulder as they swept around in a tight circle, then passed the limits of the town.

'It's wonderful,' came the eager reply. 'I'm enjoying every minute of it.'

'Well, settle back and relax, because we've got three hours of flying to do before we reach the settlement. When you get used to this I'll give you some lessons in flying. I'm sure the medical authorities will be looking for another flying nurse before very much longer. This work is becoming more organised, and if you take to the job then there's no reason why you shouldn't be the next candidate.'

'I'd really like that, Avis,' Estelle replied. 'I'm something of an individualist. I would much prefer to do this sort of thing than remain in a hospital ward. I think you're doing more good than any three nurses on the ground.'

'You sound like a girl after my own heart,' Avis said with a laugh. 'We'll see how you get along.'

Three hours soon passed away, for Estelle maintained a stream of interested questions about flying generally and the work Avis was doing around the settlements. Avis could not help but feel her own enthusiasm rekindled by the girl's zeal, and she enjoyed herself just talking about her duties and the conditions under which she worked. The more she listened to Estelle the better she liked the girl, and by the time they sighted the settlement she was more than pleased that she had the girl's company.

They made a bumpy landing, and when they alighted from the plane they found a strong wind blowing. Avis chocked the wheels and locked the cabin, and she and Estelle carried the medical cases into the hut that served as a clinic. A crowd of almost three hundred natives were waiting to be attended, and Estelle gave a gasp of amazement when she saw them.

'I'm beginning to see why you need an assistant,' she said.

'This is nothing,' Avis told her. 'Wait until we visit the larger settlements.'

'Good Lord! However have you managed to get through all the work?'

'By closing my eyes to the volume and keeping at it.' Avis suppressed a sigh as they prepared to start operation. 'I'll leave you to give out the Sabin vaccine, Estelle. I'll get the children injected. After that we'll share the duties of checking the children for trachoma and all the feet for hookworm.'

'What a job!' Estelle was still surprised. 'And you've been visiting two places a day, haven't you?'

'That's right.' Looking back on some of her busier days, Avis was beginning to wonder how she had coped with all exigencies. But that was behind her now. She organised the natives, and watched Estelle at work popping the sugar cubes soaked with pink antipolio-myelitis vaccine into the eager aboriginal mouths. Satisfied that the girl would cope, Avis went off to get on with her work, and she injected fifteen babies against whooping cough, diphtheria and tetanus.

With the babies attended to, Avis called for

168

the children with sore eyes, and a long queue of smiling, excited youngsters lined up for attention. She made a careful examination of each child, and found many cases of trachoma, mostly in its early stages thanks to her previous treatments. She issued drops for each child, and knew the doses were exactly administered by the grateful parents. After inspecting forty-three children, she discovered that only four of them showed no trace of the disease. She took their names for future reference, and by the time she was ready to start inspecting feet for hookworm Estelle appeared to inform her that she had completed the vaccine treatment.

'It took me over an hour,' the girl said.

'It's a great help to me,' Avis replied. 'That's a lot of time saved.'

'And a lot of work,' Estelle retorted. 'I feel as if I've been working all day in a ward. I wouldn't have believed that this could be so tiring.'

'And we've got another visit scheduled for this afternoon.' Avis smiled. 'Thanks to you we'll get done much earlier.'

'What do we do now?' Estelle was eager to continue, and Avis showed her what to look for in the treatment of hookworm. Between them they examined three hundred pairs of feet, and it took them until lunch. With the job completed Estelle pressed a hand to her aching back. 'I'll never know how you've been managing on your own, Avis,' she declared. 'We've been hard at it for three hours. If you had been alone it would have taken you six hours at least. There's still another visit to make.'

'Not a big one,' Avis replied. 'But if I had been alone I would have scheduled this one for today, and fitted the other in some other time.'

'I've always admired you,' Estelle went on. 'But this has opened my eyes. Anyone who envied you this job ought to be made to tackle it. They ought to give you a medal.'

'Just for doing my job?' Avis shook her head. 'There are many people doing far more important jobs than me, Estelle. I'm a very small cog in a very large machine.'

With their treatments concluded, Avis and Estelle had lunch. When they went out to the airstrip afterwards it was to find the wind very much stronger. Clouds of dust were blowing across the desolate bushland, and Estelle turned an apprehensive face to Avis.

'Will it be safe to fly, Avis?'

'At the moment it is, but if it gets any

worse we'll be grounded. I think we can make it to the next stop. But we may have to stay there overnight.' Avis glanced anxiously at the girl. 'I hope you didn't make a date for tonight,' she said slowly.

'I did, as it happens,' came the quick reply. 'But that doesn't matter. My heart and soul are in this job. David will understand if I don't show up. I warned him I was taking on this job with you.' Estelle paused. 'What about you? Did you have a date?'

'It doesn't matter about me. He can always find out where I am. We'll get on to the next place and then I'll review the situation. Hop in.'

Estelle got into the cabin, and Avis unchocked the wheels. The plane was shuddering in the wind, and for a moment Avis paused to peer around. Dust stung her face as she gauged the strength of the wind. She had flown in worse weather, and she hurried into the cabin and prepared to take-off.

The fragile machine lurched and bumped sickeningly, but they became airborne, and Avis climbed quickly above the dust. The sun was shining brightly in the upper air, but there was a great deal of wind, and Estelle showed some apprehension as the

171

plane dipped and yawed under the quickly changing pressures.

'It's a bit disconcerting,' Avis said, smiling, 'but there's nothing to worry about, Estelle.'

'It's like riding a switchback,' Estelle replied, smiling.

Avis kept a close eye on her instruments. The ground was invisible under the swirling dust clouds. But she knew her plane, and the lurching and the bumping didn't affect her in the least. There was no danger. She could fly blind, but would need to see the ground when she went down to land.

The speed of the machine was cut down by the strength of the wind, and Avis glanced at the fuel gauge. She had to remember the long flight back to Kalarra. There were now no landmarks for her in this almost featureless terrain. She trusted to her instruments, and the wind blustered against the machine as the engine throbbed powerfully.

'Do you know where we are?' Estelle suddenly demanded.

'Near enough,' Avis replied. 'Not to worry. You're really getting it on your first day, aren't you?'

'It's better to get the worst parts over with first.' There was no fear in the girl's tones.

'But it looks pretty fierce out there, Avis.'

'I'm going to have trouble setting down when we arrive,' Avis admitted. 'But the airstrips are usually pretty bare, so there won't be any danger in that shape.'

They were silent then, Avis concentrating upon her flying and Estelle considering the situation that confronted her. The storm seemed to be getting worse. There was thunder in the air, and the clouds were piling up raggedly, split intermittently by uneasy lightning. The plane staggered through the air alarmingly, and Avis threw a reassuring glance over her shoulder at Estelle, who was white-faced and tensed.

'We're getting into the heart of it,' Avis reported. 'We should be out of the worst of it by the time we reach the airstrip. It won't be long now.'

'I'm not scared, just a little nervous,' Estelle said tightly.

'Well, I'm scared,' Avis admitted with a smile. 'I don't like lightning.'

'What happens if something does go wrong?' Estelle demanded.

'We can get down all right. We have the radio. We could soon call up help. I don't think there's anything to worry about.'

'It's nice to know what the odds are,'

Estelle said slowly.

'I think you and I are going to get along very well together,' Avis told her with a smile. 'You seem to be a girl after my own heart.'

Then they were silent, and Avis began to grow tense as she realised that somewhere below them in the dust was the airstrip she was looking for. She checked her instruments, did some calculations in her mind, and considered losing altitude in an attempt to spot the strip. There was little risk of flying into anything in this area. There were hills further north, but she wouldn't have reached those even if she had miscalculated. She moistened her lips as she dived shallowly.

'Everything all right, Avis?' Estelle demanded.

'Yes. I'm going down to try and spot some landmark. We must be very near the strip now.'

'I'll hold tight then.' There was no fear in Estelle's tones, but Avis knew the girl must be on edge. This was her first day flying, and the strangeness was still with her and she hadn't yet found her confidence in the plane or its pilot. For herself, Avis was not concerned. She knew the limitations of both herself and the machine.

The dust swirled about them, and Avis dared not go lower. Now and again she caught an indistinct glimpse of the ground not far below, but there was nothing to tell her where she was. She could not pick out any feature of the area that would enable her to orientate herself. She began to consider turning and hunting for their landfall, but she knew it would be a fruitless task in the dust. They might circle until their fuel was exhausted.

'Over there, Avis,' Estelle said suddenly. 'I thought I saw some buildings.'

'Where?' Avis demanded instantly. 'Left or right?'

'Sorry! To the left.'

Avis glanced quickly in that direction, but could see nothing. She banked the machine and sent it around in a tight turn, her eyes searching the area. A moment later she saw some farm buildings.

'Good work, Estelle,' she said.

'Is it the place we're looking for?' the girl demanded.

'I don't think so, but there are several farms in the immediate area. It's now a matter of deciding which farm it is.'

She dropped lower, turning again, and they swept over the small spread of buildings. Avis narrowed her eyes as she searched for some familiar feature. Then she spotted a double barn, and turned the machine again, this time away from the buildings, watching the compass as the needle flickered around the dial.

'That's Burnett's place, I'm sure,' she said to Estelle. 'It's about five miles to the settlement and airstrip from here. Keep your eyes open, Estelle, and you may spot the place first. Anyway, full marks for your observation.'

'But you aren't far from the strip, in any event,' Estelle said. 'You flew all those miles and couldn't see a thing, but you knew where you were. I think it's marvellous.'

'I wasn't completely without aids,' Avis said with a laugh. 'This instrument panel is fitted with aids for blind flying.' She was staring ahead as she spoke, and suddenly spotted a flaring light soaring through the murk, slightly to the left and about a mile away. As it reached its apex it was in fairly clear sky. Estelle uttered a gasp when she spotted it.

'The airstrip,' Avis said. 'Someone knows we're in the area. But where did the flare come from?'

Another arose slowly, and Avis felt relief

fill her. She dropped lower, concentrating upon what she was doing. A third flare showed momentarily, and now it was exactly ahead. The ground was barely visible, and the gusting wind tried to throw the sturdy little machine off balance. Avis recognised part of the airstrip, and quickly set the plane down. She made a rather bumpy landing, staring intently around, trying to get her full bearings.

Visibility was low, almost non-existent, but she had little fear now. She knew all the strips in her area, and could land on any of them in any condition that Nature could thrust her way. But she was slightly too far to the left, and the machine was almost at a standstill when the indistinct outline of a tree appeared off the port wing.

Estelle saw it in the same instant that Avis became aware of it. The girl cried out in alarm, and Avis took evasive action instinctively. But she was too late. The wing hit the tree and the plane came to an abrupt standstill, shuddering under the impact and almost turning over. Cutting the engine, Avis took a deep breath and sat still for a moment, very near to tears. The machine was more than just a plane to her. It had character and personality. It was a living thing, a good friend, and she had damaged it. She could have cried as she hastily clambered out into the blustering wind to take stock of the damage.

CHAPTER TEN

There was a hole in the wing that made Avis catch her breath when she saw it. Dust blew into her face as she staggered forward for a closer inspection, and she held on to the wing and ran her fingers lightly over the damage. Estelle appeared at her side, frightened and tense, and the girl's voice, when she called a question, was buffeted away so that Avis had to lean sideways to catch what was said.

'Is it very bad, Avis?'

'Bad enough by the looks of it,' Avis replied. 'But we can't do anything about it now. Let's get out of this wind and see what the situation is. Perhaps we can have the plane towed into a barn out of the way. We shan't be going back to Kalarra today, Estelle.'

She kept her voice steady, although she felt very much like crying, and after chocking the wheels and locking the cabin she led the way to the nearest buildings. The wind tugged at them, as if determined to keep them from finding shelter, and Estelle grasped at Avis and they supported each other.

A figure suddenly appeared before them, running before the wind, and Avis paused, narrowing her eyes to keep the dust out of them. She recognised the figure as it approached, and her heart seemed to miss a beat as she paused. It was Ralph Curtis.

'Avis!' He was before her, grasping her shoulders and leaning close to make himself heard. 'Did you get down all right?'

'A little damage to one wing,' she retorted dully. 'Was it you firing the flares, Ralph?'

'Yes. I've been here some time. I knew you were due today, and I took advantage of the storm to ground myself. I learned by telephone that you were on your way here through the storm, and I've been out on the strip for the past hour, listening for you. Then I heard, a few moments ago, from Burnett's place, that an aeroplane had just passed over them, very low. I guessed it was you and fired the flares.'

'Thanks, Ralph. If it hadn't been for your flares then I might have missed the strip altogether.'

'Not you. I've never come across a better pilot.' He laughed harshly, and put an arm around her shoulders to steady her as the wind grew more violent. He leaned forward to peer at Estelle. 'I guess this is your assistant,' he commented. 'Not a good day for you to start your flying duties, Nurse.'

'I've enjoyed it, rather,' Estelle said, clutching at his arm. 'But I'm sorry the plane has been damaged.'

'We'll take a look at it, but not until the wind abates.' He took them by the arm and led them towards the buildings. 'It's going to rain shortly. You got here just in time, Avis. It's going to get a lot worse before it gets better.'

She made no reply. It couldn't get any worse, she thought sadly. The plane was damaged, and that was all that mattered to her. They entered the building, and Avis sighed with relief. Her ears ached from the battering of the wind, and she blinked, rubbing dust from her face and eyes. She glanced at her watch, and was surprised to find that the time was only just after three. It was afternoon, but the storm made it seem like late evening. She turned to face Ralph, who was watching her closely.

'Thanks again, Ralph,' she said slowly. 'I

always seem to be thanking you for something. What would I do without you?'

'If my memory serves me correctly you were helping me last time,' he said with a laugh. 'I'm in your debt, Avis, and don't you forget it.' He glanced at Estelle, and Avis introduced them. 'If you can get through today and still like the job then you'll be all right,' he told her.

'I do like the job,' she replied. 'And I have the greatest admiration for Avis. I have heard a lot of stories about her, but after watching her at work today I'd say they were greatly underestimated.'

'I agree with you.' He nodded emphatically. 'I thought I had a tough job until I met Avis.'

The wind was rattling the windows and shaking the door of the little building. Avis was worried about her plane.

'We've got to get to work, Estelle,' she said. 'We won't be able to leave here until the storm is over, but as soon as we get the treatments finished we can get off duty. Then I can look after the plane.'

'I think you're more interested in the plane than your patients,' Ralph said with a laugh. 'This incident is finding you out, Avis. I've often wondered which came first in your life, and now I think I know. There's not blood but oil in your veins.'

'No,' she replied. 'I'm going to attend to the patients first, Ralph.' She smiled thinly. 'The plane is only a means of transport.' It hurt her to say it, but those were her sentiments. It was clear to her that nursing was the most important thing in her life. Flying was an obsession with which she had to live. The fact that she combined both her passions gave her an advantage over most people. But nursing came first, and always would.

'I'm just pulling your leg,' Ralph said quickly. 'While you are attending to your patients I'll get your plane towed into that barn at the end of the runway. Then we can see what the damage is.'

'Would you do that? I'd be very grateful.' She smiled at him and he nodded emphatically.

'Leave it to me.' He patted her shoulder. 'I've got nothing to do, and it'll give me great pleasure to be able to do something for you.'

He departed, and Avis sighed deeply. Estelle was watching her closely, and when Avis caught the girl's eye Estelle took a deep breath.

'He's a very nice person, Avis. Have you known him long?'

'Ever since I've been on these duties,' Avis said. 'Ralph is a very dear friend, Estelle, and one of the best. I hope you'll like him as much as I do. In this business we always do what we can for each other. You never know when you may need help.'

'I've already guessed that. What shall we do now?'

'We'd better go back to the plane and get out the medical supplies. We've got some vaccine for two hundred people, and apart from a score of babies to be inoculated there are the other two regular inspections to make; trachoma and hookworm.'

'It's always the same, no matter where we go?' Estelle asked.

'That's the usual routine,' Avis agreed. 'You'll soon get used to it.'

They went back to the plane and secured their cases. Ralph appeared, and Avis gave him the keys to the machine. He promised to handle it like a baby, and Avis smiled as she and Estelle went on to the clinic. A tractor appeared, almost running them down, and it went on to tow the damaged plane into the barn.

Avis found that her mind was not

completely upon her work as she and Estelle attended to the patients. She was worried about the plane. But she forced herself to go on, and with Estelle handing out the antipoliomyelitis doses she handled the children and babies. The work was such a routine for her that she didn't need her full concentration, and her mind was busy as she looked into trusting young eyes or inspected hard black feet.

At least Ralph was here on the spot in case she should need either transport back to Kalarra or repair items brought out to her. That was one consolation, and Ralph was a very experienced airman and mechanic. If they couldn't fix the plane between them then no one could!

At last the work was over. Every native on the settlement had been treated in some way, and Avis gave a great sigh of relief as she hurried across to the barn. The wind didn't seem so strong now, but the sky was filled with storm clouds, and she fancied that rain spattered about her as she went into the barn. The door slammed at her back as she entered, and it needed all her strength to close it firmly. She had eyes only for the plane, and saw that Ralph had stripped the fabric from around the damaged wing. He was standing by the wing when she entered, and he came towards her, grinning a little as he saw the worry on her face.

'Don't look so upset,' he said softly. 'It isn't as bad as it looks. The main strut of the wing hasn't been damaged. It only needs a patch on it to make it airworthy. The thing is, what can we use from the materials on hand?'

Avis went close to the wing and stared at the damaged section. A shuddering sigh gusted through her with the relief that came. There was no serious damage! She could have kissed Ralph as she turned to him. He was smiling gently, watching her face closely.

'I've got some sterile towels and bandages,' she said slowly. 'With some sticking plaster, I'm sure I can patch it up good enough to get back to Kalarra.'

He stared at her for a moment, surprise showing on his face. Then he nodded and laughed. 'You're the very limit, Avis! I don't know why I bother to try and help you. I've never seen a more self-sufficient girl. I've been standing here for more than an hour, racking my brains over the best way to fix this damage, and you take one look at it and come up with a near perfect idea. How do you do it?'

'That was easy.' She smiled. 'If I came

across someone with a hole in his leg I'd bandage it, wouldn't I? So what's so different about a hole in the wing of a plane?'

'There's logical reasoning for you,' he said, grinning. 'Okay, go and get the first aid kit and we'll see what we can do.'

She hurried to the door, and he called to her, coming up behind. He opened the door for her, using his strength, and Avis was very close to him as she slipped out through the narrow opening. For a moment their glances met, and she saw a flash of desire in his pale eyes. Then his lips tightened and he grinned.

'Knock when you want to come back in,' he said in her ear. 'This door is too big for you to handle.'

She nodded and departed, and almost ran across to the clinic. She was breathless when she reached the little building, and Estelle looked up when Avis entered.

'Can you fix it?' the girl demanded.

'I think so.' Avis gasped for breath. 'I need sticking plaster, bandages and sterile towels, Estelle.'

'Is someone hurt?' the girl demanded in alarmed tones.

'Only the plane,' Avis retorted, laughing. 'Come and watch my brand of surgery. It will be something for you to tell your children when they start coming along.'

Going back to the barn, Avis set to work with great enterprise, patching the damaged wing with the items of first aid. Ralph stood by watching intently, and when she had finished he shook his head doubtfully. Avis moved to his side and waited for his comments.

'That should hold it,' she said.

'If you don't try to take off until the storm is over! You wouldn't be so mad as to attempt it, would you?'

'No.' Avis shook her head. 'The plane is a patient now. I wouldn't try anything that might add to its damage.'

'You should be thinking of your neck, and Estelle's,' he said quickly. 'If the wing came off at a thousand feet what would you do?'

'Crash-land.' She smiled. 'What would you do?'

He shook his head. 'You never cease to amaze me, Avis. I'm not leaving here until I've seen you into the air.'

'It looks as if we'll be grounded until tomorrow at the very earliest,' she said. 'I'm sorry about your date tonight, Estelle.'

'That's the very least of my worries,' the girl retorted.

'Me, too!' Avis sighed as she went forward to examine the patch. 'I think we'll be airworthy tomorrow. Anyway, we'll try it out in the morning and find out.'

'Be careful,' Ralph warned. 'It would break my heart if anything happened to you, Avis.'

She nodded, collecting together the items of equipment she had been using. 'You don't have to worry about me, Ralph,' she told him. 'I can take care of myself.'

'I know that only too well.' There was a trace of bitterness in his tones which caused her to glance quickly at him. But he was already looking towards Estelle. 'Well, would you like to see a real plane?' he demanded. 'I fly a two-engined cargo plane. It would swallow Avis's bird with no trouble at all. Come with me and look it over.'

'I'd love to, if it's all right with Avis,' Estelle replied.

'Go ahead,' Avis told her, smiling. 'It's about time you had a break today. But be careful. Ralph will bore you to tears with his old flying tales.'

'Don't you believe her,' he retorted, grinning. 'Come on, Estelle, and see how real fliers get around.'

Avis went back to the clinic, and she

sighed her relief when she could sit down and relax. But her nerves were too tense to give her much rest. She telephoned the hospital at Kalarra and reported the situation. A weather report gave her hopes for flying early next day, and she wondered about the patched hole in her port wing. It would be better to fly without Estelle, just in case, and she wondered if Ralph would be going straight back to Kalarra in the morning.

She had hardly hung up when the phone rang, and lifting the receiver, she heard Duncan's voice in her ear.

'Avis, are you all right?' he demanded worriedly. 'I asked the switchboard to let me know as soon as you reported in. What happened to you? There was some sort of accident, wasn't there?'

'Nothing to worry about,' she retorted, forcing a laugh to reassure him. 'I knocked a hole in the port wing. It's been patched, so you can forget about it.'

'That's something I won't be able to do. Avis, I've been worried stiff all day. Why didn't you stay here, knowing there was bad weather coming up?'

'Because I have my work to do.' She shook her head slowly. 'I've made two visits today. It's progress, you know.'

189

'But one day wouldn't make any difference, Avis,' he argued. 'I've had visions of you lying shattered in the wreckage of that machine. Are you sure you're all right?'

'Positive!' She relished his concern. There was a warmth inside her that came just because she could hear his voice. 'Duncan,' she said softly. 'If it's any help, I've missed you today.'

'You have?' He laughed lightly. 'That makes all my worrying worthwhile. Just wait until you get back!'

'What will you do?' she demanded.

'Kiss you breathless, or something. But I have news for you, Avis. I'm taking over as mobile doctor from Merrick Ramsey. I've been bitten by the bug, you might say. If you're going to have this passion for flying all your life then I'd better join you, because I know I'll never be able to beat it.'

'Duncan, you haven't!' Her surprise sounded clearly in her tones.

'Why not? Don't you know yet that I'll do anything for you?'

'Yes, I know. I'm grateful for the knowledge. I'm beginning to see everything a little more clearly now. I realise that I've been living under a strain for weeks, and it was slowly getting worse. Having an assistant has eased the pressure. Do me a favour, will you?'

'Anything you say!'

'Ask me out tomorrow evening, and let's go somewhere quiet, where we can enjoy our own company.'

'Avis!' His tones were sharp again. 'Are you sure you're all right?'

'I've never felt better.' She nodded slowly. 'I love you, Duncan, more than anything in the world.'

'Here, steady on! That's a pretty sweeping statement. What about nursing? What about your flying?'

'If I had a choice to make between the three – flying, nursing and you, do you know which I'd choose?' There was a light-hearted inflection in her voice.

'I daren't even try to guess,' he replied.

'Then I'll tell you.' She paused, smiling, suddenly feeling light-hearted as she had never done before. It was as if she had reached and passed a crisis in her sub-conscious mind. The fact that it was over was obvious to her, but the reasons for it were obscured. Yet she felt that the first shaft of true love had pierced her shell and made its presence known. It had to be that. She was in love and could now understand it.

The doubts that had arisen when Ralph kissed her had come from inexperience. She had never been in love before and hadn't known what to expect. But she knew now. In some intangible way the knowledge had come to her.

'I'm waiting, Avis,' Duncan said sharply. 'Are you still there?'

'Sorry!' She laughed. 'I was thinking.'

'Surely it isn't as hard as all that to make a decision.'

'No. I sidetracked myself. I don't have to hesitate at all. You're the most important, Duncan. You and your love.'

'I never really expected to hear those words from you,' he admitted. 'When will you be back, Avis? Some time tomorrow?'

'During the morning. I'll take off here if the weather permits. I've got to come back for another schedule and some more supplies.'

'I'm likely to be out on a call, you know, but in case I don't see you then let's make some tentative arrangements. I'll pick you up at the Home at seven. Think you can make that?'

'Nothing will stop me,' she retorted.

'Good. I'll treat it with the same urgency.' He laughed. 'I love you, Avis, and it's a great pity a storm is keeping us apart this evening.'

'It won't last forever,' she said softly. 'I'll be back tomorrow. The time will soon pass.'

'I'll be counting every minute.' He was cheerful now. 'I won't be able to see you soon enough. I've had some very bad doubts about us during the past few days, although I've said nothing to you about them.'

'You have?' She caught her breath as she waited for him to go on.

'Yes. About Ralph Curtis. I had a strange feeling that he was my rival for you. It seemed to me that you couldn't make up your mind between the two of us.'

'It must have been your imagination, Duncan,' she said in quiet tones. 'There has never been any real doubt in my mind about you. I told you I like Ralph, and he's proved himself a great friend. But it never went any deeper than that.'

'I didn't believe you the first time you told me,' he admitted. 'But I believe you now, Avis; you'll never know just how much I love you.'

'I do have a good idea,' she said. 'Look for me tomorrow, Duncan. I'll get back as soon as I can.'

'I'll be waiting. Goodbye now, and be very

careful in the morning, won't you?'

'I'll take care.' She rang off and hung up slowly, her mind filled with thoughts of him, and she knew without doubt that what she had told him was the truth. She was in love with him, and she would never have misgivings again.

The wind rattled the windows, and she felt a shiver pass through her slim body. But the future seemed very bright indeed! A deep and satisfying happiness was beginning to manifest itself in her. Anticipation heightened her senses, and excitement ran wild through her veins. This was being in love, she told herself silently. This strange and wonderful upheaval of her life and values. She felt suddenly like a child tottering alone on the brink of a precipice, but she wouldn't have changed the sensation for anything in the world. So long as Duncan was there in the background then everything would be all right...

CHAPTER ELEVEN

Later Avis sought out Ralph, leaving Estelle in the small room in the clinic which was at their disposal. She found him in his aeroplane at the end of the runway. He was seated in the cargo bay, staring out through the open hatch, and dust was whirling about the machine. He reached out a hand and pulled her aboard, smiling as she gasped for breath. He slammed the hatch shut, and the interior of the plane was shadowed.

'Come into the cabin,' he said. 'It'll be more comfortable.'

Avis followed him, and she sat in the co-pilot's seat, next to him. The aircraft was shuddering under the pressures being exerted by the wind, and Avis sighed as she relaxed in the seat.

'I was hoping to see you,' he said conversationally. 'I had your new assistant in here for some time, and she's as keen as you on flying. I had to explain all the controls, and she'll even go flying with me on her day off if I let her.'

'Enthusiasm is a great thing,' Avis said, suppressing a sigh. 'Would you have gone far without it, Ralph?'

'No.' He shook his head. 'But disillusionment set in rather early with me, Avis.' He glanced at her, a tight smile upon his handsome face. 'I don't think you've been disillusioned yet, have you?'

'I hope I shall never be,' she retorted.

'You deserve better than that,' he agreed. 'You're the most unselfish girl I've ever come across. I had hopes of making you my wife, Avis. I would have been proud and happy to the very end if it had worked out that way.'

'I'm sorry, truly sorry, Ralph,' she replied slowly. 'I've always liked you a great deal.'

'But liking isn't enough, and there's a doctor waiting for you back in Kalarra.' He sighed deeply, his skilled hands pulling on the controls of the machine. 'It's going to take me a long time to get over you, Avis, unless–!' He paused and stared at her for a moment, his pale eyes glinting. 'Unless you haven't quite made up your mind about Duncan Ross yet. Is there any hope for me?'

'None at all! I hate to have to tell you, but Duncan telephoned earlier, after I had reported the situation to Kalarra. I told him

I loved him, Ralph.'

'And you've spoken the truth. You do love him.' He nodded. 'I hope he knows just how fortunate he is.'

'I think he does, Ralph.'

'I'm sure he does. Well, that leaves me with precious little to say, eh? Except congratulations.' He leaned towards her and took her hand in his. 'I wish you every happiness, Avis. I hope you'll never regret taking this step. It will mean changing or adapting your life considerably, and I hope you can manage it all right.'

'I think I can.' She spoke in low tones, sorry for him, knowing that he would be feeling pain at his failure to interest her.

'Well, good luck!' He spoke firmly. 'It's been a real pleasure knowing you, Avis. They'll never be able to completely replace you.'

'But I'm not finishing yet,' she said.

'You will one day. You won't be able to go on. Love will make some major changes in your life. Will you be able to face up to them?'

'I'm ready to. I have considered them.'

'Well, I don't think I would be able to give anything up. I love the way I live.' He smiled. 'Perhaps it's just as well that you didn't fall for me, Avis. It would have been a pretty complicated life.'

'It's good of you to make so light of it. But I can tell by your face that it affects you a great deal more than you're showing.'

'Then you're seeing far more than you ought, and it's time to call a halt.' He stirred impatiently in his seat. 'Do you think you could fly this old crate?' he demanded.

'Certainly.' She replied instantly, prepared to go along with his change of subject. 'It's a lot heavier than my plane, but it shouldn't be too difficult.'

'You need fifty per cent more runway and speed on this. That's about all. Two engines are as simple as one.'

'Show me the controls,' she said. 'I never miss the opportunity to learn something about flying.'

For more than an hour Ralph sat at her side, teaching her the theory of flying the big machine, and Avis was intent upon picking up all the details. She was always hungry to gain new information about flying, and if there hadn't been a storm in progress she would have begged him to let her fly the plane. He was happy talking about flying, and Avis was quite content to listen. But when he had exhausted the subject he changed to his personal view once more.

'Avis, doesn't this prove that you and I are very much alike?' he demanded. 'Would anyone believe that we passed the last hour talking about flying this old crate?' He laughed thinly. 'I wish you would fall in love with me.'

'It won't help either of us to go over that again, Ralph,' she said. 'It hurts me to know that you feel pain because of what's happening. Perhaps it would be better if we didn't see one another again for a spell.'

'That might hurt me even more,' he said. 'I don't know what the answer is, I can tell you. I've had a few sleepless nights lately, with you on my mind.'

'When I leave tomorrow we'll try and stay out of each other's way,' she said firmly. 'It will be for your sake as well as mine.'

'I'll try your machine in the morning, before you set off back to Kalarra,' he said. 'I'm not going to let you risk your pretty neck in a patched-up crate, Avis.'

'I think the patch will hold,' she replied. 'I'll do my own testing, Ralph. If anything should go wrong it ought to be my neck that suffers. I patched the hole.'

'Your neck is too precious,' he retorted.

Avis got to her feet, stifling a sigh. He hurried ahead of her, opening the hatch. He grinned as she jumped to the ground.

'Don't get blown away, Avis,' he said. 'See you in the morning.'

'Where are you sleeping tonight?' she demanded, having to shout to make herself heard.

'In here, of course. It won't be the first time, I can tell you.'

She nodded and turned away, shielding her face and eyes from the raging dust. Her mind was seething with turmoil. The more she thought about Duncan the clearer came her knowledge that she loved him, but she was racked by the awareness that Ralph was being hurt because of her love for Duncan. Ever sensitive, she was appalled by the thought that someone was suffering through an action of hers.

Back in the little room, she faced Estelle without expression. The girl had settled down on the camp bed in the corner and was reading a magazine. She dropped the book and sat up to look at Avis.

'You have to spend many nights away from Kalarra like this?' the girl demanded.

'Not many. This is just one of those unforeseen circumstances. Occasionally I do make an overnight stop when I have a lot of work to do, but usually I arrange things so I get back to town after a day out in the bush.'

'So I'm just unlucky in that my first trip coincides with an unforeseen circumstance,' Estelle said with a laugh. 'Shall we be able to fly back to Kalarra tomorrow?'

'I expect so. The storm is expected to die during the night. I'll test the plane in the morning to see if the patch holds, and then we'll be on our way back.'

'I wouldn't want to be stuck in a place like this for weeks on end,' the girl went on.

'There was some talk a while back that a trained nurse ought to live in on each settlement.' Avis smiled as Estelle cringed in mock horror. 'It doesn't bear thinking about, does it?'

Estelle agreed, and they settled down to pass the long evening. The wind showed no signs of abating, and when they finally turned in, the windows were still rattling under the furious onslaughts from Nature. Avis went to sleep almost immediately, her mind tired out by the bubbling emotions that had rioted through her during the long day. The night was peaceful, and during it the wind did drop.

The powerful roar of an aeroplane engine brought Avis out of her sleep, and she sat up in bed before she was fully awake, frowning as she recognised the sound of the engine. It belonged to her plane. She jumped out of the bed and padded across the floor in her bare feet to peer from the window, and she gasped when she saw her machine speeding along the bumpy track, racing to gain flying speed.

'What is it?' Estelle's voice was almost inaudible against the noise of the plane.

'Ralph is testing the plane.' Avis turned away from the window and hurriedly began to dress. 'I'd forgotten I'd given him the keys yesterday. He didn't return them, and he said he wouldn't let me test the plane myself.'

'I like him. He's a thoroughly genuine man.' Estelle was dressing furiously, but Avis left her behind as she hurried from the building. Outside, she found the wind had gone completely, and her plane was airborne, soaring high into the brilliant sky. Natives were hurrying from all directions to watch, and Avis stood breathless as she watched.

Ralph took the machine to a thousand feet and began to perform a series of loops and rolls destined to test the airworthiness of the plane. He could certainly handle the machine, Avis thought, and she was interested in the progress he made across the sky. The plane was safe enough for the trip back to Kalarra, she thought.

Estelle joined her, and stared spellbound at the tricks Ralph was performing. Avis narrowed her blue eyes. Ralph was doing more than testing the machine. He was showing off. He came in a steep dive, straight towards the buildings, and Avis watched in critical wonder. The sun glinted on the powerful machine and the roar of its engine closed across the bush. Quick as a flash Ralph sped by, soaring up again until the plane became a speck in the brilliance, and Avis had to shield her eyes to pick him out of the glare.

'He's done enough,' she said slowly, and there was a faint throbbing in her ears. 'That patch won't stand too much strain. It should carry us safely back to Kalarra, but there's an enormous amount of strain being placed upon it by all those aerobatics.'

'He's a good pilot,' Estelle said hopefully. 'He knows how far he can go.'

They watched for several moments, but there was no sign of Ralph. The engine noise had faded away and the early morning was peaceful again. Avis waited tensely, wondering, hoping Ralph would soon return, but he did not appear.

'Where's he gone?' Estelle demanded.

'There's only one way to find out.' Avis started towards Ralph's machine, down at the near end of the airstrip. Estelle hurried to keep pace with her.

'What are you going to do?' the girl asked.

'Call him up on his radio.' Avis was almost running to the parked machine, her intuition at work, her eyes narrowed with foreboding.

When they reached the plane they clambered aboard, and Avis found her hands trembling as she entered the large cabin and switched on the power. The radio was simple enough to use, and she called Ralph, peering through the windows in the hope of seeing him somewhere in the nearby sky, but there was no sign of him. She kept calling, and there was no reply.

'Do you think something has happened to him?' Estelle asked in frightened tones.

'Not to Ralph. He just hasn't got my radio on receive. It's a rule of the air that radios are left on receive. But he knows the first thing I'll do is call him up, so he's switched to transmit so he can't hear me.'

'What's got into him?' Estelle stared at the sky, leaning across the controls in an attempt to get a clear view.

'Nothing. He's just doing a more than thorough job on my plane,' Avis retorted.

They waited for some time, and Avis called on the radio until her throat ached. When she was certain that he wasn't going to answer she switched off the power and left the plane. Estelle jumped to the ground behind her.

'He should have returned by now,' Estelle said worriedly. 'You don't think something might have happened to him, do you?'

'I don't know what to think.' Avis stood on the runway and studied the sky, her head canted to one side so that her ears could pick up the first sound of an approaching plane. The silence seemed to throb, and several times she imagined she heard her engine, but there was no sign of the aircraft.

It was fifteen minutes after Ralph had disappeared that Avis came to a decision. She stared around the airstrip, and sent Estelle to clear away the watching natives.

'What are you going to do?' Estelle asked doubtfully.

'I'm going to fly Ralph's plane, to look for him,' Avis retorted firmly.

Estelle flashed her a look of alarm, but went off nevertheless to follow Avis's bidding. For a few moments more Avis stood looking around, straining her ears for sound of her plane, but the silence seemed to mock her, and she let her pent-up breath go with a long sigh. Getting back into Ralph's plane, she entered the cabin and sat down in the pilot's seat. For a few moments she concentrated on what Ralph had told her the previous evening. Then she began to go through the procedure of starting the engines. She was tense as first one engine, then the other, fired. The noise was not like anything she had ever experienced before, and her nerve almost failed her. But a glance around at the empty sky spurred her on and she knew that something bad had happened to Ralph.

She saw Estelle standing at the side of the runway, and the girl was searching the skies for sign of the missing plane. Avis switched on the radio and called again, but silence remained, and the emptiness of the sky proclaimed that Ralph had met with some untoward incident.

When she was ready for take-off Avis stared along the runway, judging the distance. In her own machine she could have taken off in a blindfold and still handled the plane perfectly, but this cumbersome old crate, and old it was, could not be compared with her own lighter aircraft.

She stepped up the power to the engines, then throttled down again and hurried through the cargo bay, dropping to the ground outside to remove the wheel chocks. Her lips were thin and firm as she returned to the cabin. This time she took the engines up step by step, until the machine seemed to be shuddering with eagerness and impatience. Avis could feel her heart thumping madly as the plane began to move. The runway seemed bumpier than she could ever remember it, and they gathered speed so slowly. She remembered all that Ralph had told her, and was thankful that her natural curiosity had made her pick up most of the important details last evening. She tensed as she reached flying speed, and slowly the nose lifted and became airborne.

Once in the air she lost her tension, and sent the large plane up into the sky. Then she began to circle, staring at the bushland for signs of her own machine. She dreaded what she might discover, but she had to search, and now she could only believe that Ralph had tried one trick too many and had crashed.

In ever widening circles she searched the area around the airstrip, and as she got farther away from the runway her spirits began to rise. There was no sign of a crashed plane. Perhaps she had been worrying for nothing. Ralph might have gone on a short flight to further test the damaged wing. She breathed steadily, fighting to control her emotions. But in the back of her mind a dull pang of intuition tried to overpower her optimism.

Then she spotted her plane. It lay crumpled like a shot bird at the end of a short path which it had cleared for itself in the bush. Shock speared through her and tears started in her eyes. Turning a little, she swooped low, passing over the spot, and one hand went out to the radio. She could see the left wing of her plane was just unrecognisable wreckage, and there was no sign of Ralph. He had crash landed, judging by the tell-tale marks behind the plane, and the shortness of the skid testified to the steep angle of impact. She tore her eyes from the scene and gained height, checking the position of the crash, and she was frozen inside with horror and shock.

Calling Kalarra, she gave details to be passed on to the police, and asked for the emergency services to be alerted. She promised to land and check the damage, then report again. Cutting radio contact, she banked sharply and headed back to the airstrip.

As she landed Estelle came running towards the plane, and Avis tried to control her shock as she jumped to the ground and ran towards the nurse. Estelle took one look at her face and guessed the truth. Before the girl could say anything Avis spoke quickly.

'Get the first aid kit, Estelle, quickly. There's been a crash.'

The girl nodded and hurried away, and Avis looked around, still partially stunned by what had happened. But she was not concerned with her machine. Ralph was out there alone, probably very badly injured and needing expert aid. A Land-Rover came up, driven by a native, and Avis climbed in beside the driver. When Estelle returned with the first aid box she scrambled into the vehicle at Avis's side, and the driver sent the Land-Rover forward under Avis's directions.

There was silence in the vehicle. Avis was stunned by what had happened. She could not get her thoughts moving. All her actions were instinctive. Estelle was dumb at her side, her knuckles showing white where she gripped the handle of the large red-cross box. The vehicle lurched and bumped madly across uneven ground, and Avis stared ahead, her mind picking out the direction, and every detail of the crash was emblazoned fierily across the broad screen of her mind. When she thought they were nearing the spot where Ralph had come down she leaned forward to peer through the dusty windscreen, and soon she saw the skid marks where her beloved plane had first touched down.

The driver followed the marks, and Avis saw that bushes had been uprooted and the ground furrowed. Ahead lay the crumpled wreckage, and the driver brought the vehicle to a halt some yards short of it. Estelle tumbled out with the red-cross box, and Avis stepped down and started forward on trembling legs.

Her machine was tilted over to the port side, the wing snapped and crumpled, and the tail of the plane was in the air, the nose buried deeply in loose ground. The door of the cabin had burst open with the force of the impact, and Avis could see Ralph's head showing. He was lolling in the cabin, hunched over the controls.

'Do you think he's dead?' Estelle broke the

heavy silence with her trembling tones, and Avis shook herself from the paralysis that seemed to grip her. Glancing at Estelle's stricken face, she took a deep breath.

'We'll soon know, Estelle.' Her lips moved stiffly and she found difficulty in pronouncing her words crisply. She had to force herself to fight the urge to run to the plane. A glance around showed her the driver of the Land-Rover standing by the front of his vehicle, and Avis nodded to herself. She had further need of him.

When she reached the plane she paused and looked at it as if she had never seen it before. Estelle halted at her side, evidently waiting for her to do something. Avis tightened her lips and climbed up on the starboard wing, now reared up towards the brassy sky, and she slid towards the cabin, dropping to her knees only feet away from the motionless head of Ralph Curtis. She leaned against the side of the cabin and gently touched Ralph's head. There was no movement from Ralph. His head was limp upon his neck.

Easing herself forward a little more, Avis gently lifted his head, trying to get a look at him for signs of injury. There was a large bump in the centre of his forehead, and she shook her head slowly when she realised that he hadn't strapped himself into the seat. What had come over him? The question was large in her mind as her professional instincts took over. She felt for a pulse, and overwhelming relief surged through her when she felt one. It was weak and erratic but it was there!

'He's still alive, Estelle,' she called curtly.

'Thank God!' There was no mistaking the fervent prayer in the girl's tremulous voice.

'Can you get around to the other side and help me ease him back? I want to check his limbs before we attempt to move him.'

Estelle moved around, and the machine dipped ominously as she put her weight upon the broken wing.

'Steady,' Avis called quickly. 'It won't take much to turn her completely over.'

Estelle's intent face appeared opposite, and Avis slid back the canopy roof, experiencing a little difficulty at first. Then they leaned in over the unconscious man and moved him back from the controls. His head slumped back and Estelle held him. Avis looked into his face for a moment, then felt for his heartbeat. It seemed steady enough, and she took a deep breath as she began to check him superficially for damaged limbs.

'His left arm is broken,' she said at length, and her glance met Estelle's for a moment. 'Try and hold him steady. I'm more worried about his ribs. We're going to have to try and get him out of here.'

She checked his legs, and her teeth clicked together when she found a large swelling just below his left knee.

'There's a break here,' she said.

'Left humerus broken; left tibia broken,' Estelle said in sombre tones, as if she were in the Casualty Department of the hospital. She watched Avis intently, her face taut and pale with shock. 'His nose has been bleeding, Avis,' she said suddenly.

'I'll come to that in a moment,' Avis replied. She checked Ralph's right leg, but found no sign of damage. Then she started checking his body, and her nimble, gentle fingers probed and searched for injuries. She glanced at Estelle when she believed there was no bodily damage, and she nodded slightly in answer to the question in the girl's worried eyes.

'He's taken a nasty crack on the head,' Estelle said. She was supporting Ralph's head, and her face was very close to his.

'I don't like the look of that area on his

forehead,' Avis replied. 'I'll hold him now, Estelle, while you get the bandages. We'll have to strap his arm before we can move him. That leg is going to present us with a greater difficulty.'

'We could bind a stick to it until we get him out,' Estelle said helpfully, jumping to the ground. She opened the first aid box and took out a triangular bandage, folding it quickly and rejoining Avis. Between them they managed to put the bandage on Ralph, making a sling of it and pinning the injured arm gently across his chest.

Avis was only concerned with getting him out of the plane. Other natives were arriving now, but they stood back at a distance, and Avis dropped to the ground to find a stick suitable for bandaging to Ralph's fractured leg.

'One would think my experience would have taught me always to carry splints in the plane,' she said through her clenched teeth when she had rejoined Estelle. The stick she had procured hardly seemed strong enough for what she wanted. But it would have to do.

'You can't think of everything,' Estelle said gently.

Avis smiled thinly and turned to call over

some of the native men. They came readily when they knew they could be of use, and Avis had two of them take Ralph's weight. They lifted him half out of the cabin and she and Estelle managed to bind the stick to the injured leg. Then Ralph was lifted clear and placed gently upon a stretcher brought from the clinic. As he was lifted into the back of the Land-Rover Avis glanced at her plane. But she was not concerned with it now. She had a patient to attend.

They got Ralph back to the clinic, and she sent a call through to the hospital at Kalarra, reporting the extent of Ralph's injuries and mentioning that she suspected he had a fracture of the skull. The call was put through to the mobile doctor, and Avis heard the beloved voice of Duncan in her ear. He was very worried, and didn't concern himself with the patient.

'Were you involved in the accident, Avis?' he demanded.

'No. I'm all right, Duncan. But Ralph is unconscious and seriously hurt.'

'It will take me four hours to get to you,' he replied.

'And four hours to get him back to Kalarra.' Her voice was sharp and stilted. 'If he has fractured his skull you'll probably

215

have to do a decompression on him, and time is important. I could fly him back to Kalarra in his own plane, Duncan. That would save four hours.'

'But you can't fly that great thing.'

'I did this morning. I have no fears on that part of it. But the take-off will be bumpy. Do you think we should risk it?'

'Yes.' He spoke without hesitation. 'Time is vital. Get him here as soon as you can, Avis. I'll have an ambulance standing by at the airport when you get there.' He paused. 'The hospital field will be too small for you, won't it?'

'Yes.' Her throat ached with constriction. 'I'll keep in touch by radio on the way in, Duncan, just in case there's a crisis in Ralph's condition. I'd better go now.'

'Happy landings!' His voice could not remain free of worry. 'I'll have everything ready for you at this end.'

She hung up quickly, pushing her personal thoughts into the background of her mind. The preparations for the mercy flight were simple. She had a camp bed placed in the cargo bay of the plane and Ralph was strapped to it. He was in shock, and Estelle tended him while Avis prepared for take-off. But the girl called Avis just before they were

216

ready to leave and, fearing the worst, Avis hurried into the cargo bay, to find Ralph's eyes flickering. She dropped to one knee beside him as he came partially to consciousness, and her heart seemed to miss a beat when he recognised her.

'Avis.' The word was more like a whisper on his thin lips.

'Please don't talk, Ralph,' she commanded. 'You're badly hurt, and must rest until I can get you into hospital.'

'I just want to say that your plane isn't airworthy.' A ghost of a smile touched his lips. 'I'm glad it was me tested it and not you.' His eyes closed and his voice trailed away. But he made the effort to speak again before slipping back into oblivion. 'I once said the only way I would get your full attention was by falling ill, Avis. I suppose this is the next best thing!'

She stared down at his relaxed face, and tears shimmered in her eyes. Estelle reached out and patted her arm, and Avis pulled herself from her thoughts and went back into the cabin. She began the preparation to take-off, and minutes later the large machine bumped along the runway and lifted into the air. As she headed towards distant Kalarra, Avis glanced down at the bushland and saw the crumpled wreckage that had been her plane. But there was no emotion inside her now. For the very first time in her life everything that mattered to her was properly in proportion. She knew without doubt that Duncan came first, then nursing, and lastly her flying. A small sense of satisfaction filled her as she flew unerringly towards the town. It was as if some nagging irritation of her subconscious mind had finally found relief.

As the hours passed she lost herself to the automatic mental condition needed for flying. Instincts took over to combat the fatigue that grew with sitting still and concentrating upon the panel of instruments. There was no sensation of movement, just a ceaseless vigil, with the never-ending noise of the powerful engines battering her ears.

Estelle came through shortly before they reached Kalarra, and the girl reported there was no change in Ralph's condition. Avis took that as a hopeful sign, and called Kalarra airport, alerting them as to the estimated time of her arrival. Soon they were sighting the town, and moments later Avis put the large machine down on the smooth concrete of the runway. Hardly before they stopped rolling there was an ambulance coming alongside, and within moments Ralph had been transferred and was on his way to hospital.

Avis and Estelle travelled in the ambulance, and when they reached the hospital Avis went to report to Miss Anson. She felt as if she were in a bad dream. Reality seemed far away. She hardly heard what Matron had to say, but she gathered that she was off duty for the rest of the day.

'I hope this incident won't upset you too much, Avis,' Miss Anson said softly. 'I've already made a telephone report of this to the Medical Authorities, and they think they can borrow a plane for you until yours is repaired. But we can talk about that later. You'd better get some rest. It's been a nasty ordeal for you.'

Avis nodded and took her leave, but she went down to the casualty department, and there she saw Duncan, waiting for her. He came swiftly towards her, his face intent, his eyes showing his deep feelings. As he put his arms protectively around her shoulders Avis felt some of her weakness flee. She looked up into his face.

'It's all right, Avis,' he said gently. 'I've just come out of Theatre. Ralph is going to be all right. If you hadn't brought him in there would have been a crisis, but they got him in there in time.' He paused, searching her face. 'You're looking very shocked yourself. Are you upset at losing your plane?'

'No. That hasn't entered my head at all.' She smiled slowly. 'Does that surprise you? It does me! I always thought flying my passion, but when it came to the test I discovered that people mean more to me than an assembly of metal.'

'I've often wondered about that,' he said, smiling. 'But there is no doubt that you have your heart in the right place, Avis.'

'And that heart belongs to you,' she whispered. 'I love you, Duncan. Being able to think of you during the past hours has kept me going. Without you in the background I'm sure I would never have coped.'

'You'll never have the chance to find out about that,' he said with great satisfaction. 'I'm going to be in your life for always, and not just in the background. The past hours have been dreadful for me, Avis. I've been worried sick, not knowing exactly what had happened. But it helped to clear my mind, as it has cleared yours. I think we both can see the direction for the future.'

'The direction doesn't matter,' she replied, relaxing slowly. 'So long as we're together then nothing else can matter. Don't you agree?'

His answer was to take her in his arms, regardless of the nurses around, and to kiss her soundly. Even when Matron appeared and passed them he did not release her.

'It's about time,' Miss Anson said softly, in passing, and Avis gasped in shock.

But Duncan grinned as he looked around. 'You'll be invited to the wedding, Matron,' he said.

Avis smiled too, and his words remained in her mind, a balm for the shock that still lingered there. Then he kissed her again, and she knew perfect peace.

'Will I get an invitation, too?' she demanded.

'We'll invite each other,' he said, and led her out of the hospital, taking her towards the Nurses' Home, and he paused very frequently to kiss her.

The publishers hope that this book has given you enjoyable reading. Large Print Books are especially designed to be as easy to see and hold as possible. If you wish a complete list of our books please ask at your local library or write directly to:

Dales Large Print Books
Magna House, Long Preston,
Skipton, North Yorkshire.
BD23 4ND

This Large Print Book, for people
who cannot read normal print,
is published under the auspices of

THE ULVERSCROFT FOUNDATION